'Penny, I want you,' Dominic exclaimed hoarsely. 'A wanting that began almost from the first moment I saw you. . .and I knew it would be like this, almost from that first moment. Just as you knew it too, didn't you, Penny?'

'Yes, I want you,' she stated tonelessly. 'Even I'm not stupid enough to try denying that. But no, unlike you, I. . .I happen to believe there has to be something more than the mere gratifying of a physical urge.'

'Has there?' he drawled. 'I really wouldn't know.' He rolled from her on to his back and lay gazing up at the ceiling.

'No, you wouldn't, would you?' she exclaimed bitterly, a bitterness she found oddly devoid of any sense of humiliation but, far more oddly, based on an elusive and completely inexplicable sense of disappointment.

WE HOPE you're enjoying our new addition to our Contemporary Romance series—stories which take a light-hearted look at the Zodiac and show that love can be written in the stars!

Every month you can get to know a different combination of star-crossed lovers, with one story that follows the fortunes of a hero or heroine when they embark on the romance of a lifetime with somebody born under another sign of the Zodiac. This month features a sizzling love-affair between **Libra** and **Leo**.

To find out more fascinating facts about this month's featured star sign, turn to the back pages of this book. . .

ABOUT THIS MONTH'S AUTHOR

Kate Proctor says: 'I admit to being a typical Sagittarian. With an abundance of other Fire signs in my life—including a Leo elder daughter—only too happy to help lead me astray, I'm eternally grateful for the gently sobering presence of my Virgo younger daughter. . .and my readers too, because sharing my fantasies with them is what I love most.'

FORTUNE IN THE STARS

BY

KATE PROCTOR

MILLS & BOON LIMITED
ETON HOUSE   18–24 PARADISE ROAD
RICHMOND   SURREY   TW9 1SR

First published in Great Britain 1991
by Mills & Boon Limited

© Kate Proctor 1991

Australian copyright 1991
Philippine copyright 1991
This edition 1991

ISBN 0 263 77245 4

STARSIGN ROMANCES is a trademark of Harlequin Enterprises B.V., Fribourg Branch. Mills and Boon is an authorised user.

Set in 10 on 11 pt Linotron Times
01-9109-56052 Z
Typeset in Great Britain by Centracet, Cambridge
Made and printed in Great Britain

CHAPTER ONE

LAVISH floodlighting swelled the moonlight bathing the villa coming into sight as Penny Elliot rounded the last of the hairpin bends along the road leading towards the Formentor Peninsula. Her sigh of relief was audible as she turned up the long drive approaching the gracefully Moorish outlines of a large and dazzlingly white house. She had been mentally prepared for something a lot smaller, she realised with a wry smile of affection; Lexy Raphael's description of the place had been characteristically vague but, she supposed, by the standards of the fabled wealth of the Raphael family, this palace looming up ahead of her was probably something they would regard as cramped.

Penny winced as the car hit a sleeping policeman, Lexy's voice echoing in her ears as she hurriedly changed gear.

'Penelope Elliot, you're twenty-three years old, a knockout to look at and, despite this temporary set-back, the world will return to being your oyster in a few weeks—just you wait and see!'

'I suppose "temporary set-back" is one way of putting it.' Penny's own jaundiced reply returned to her. 'Having been made redundant on Monday and today losing the roof from over my head with the discovery that the man who claims to want to marry me is having an affair with my flatmate. . . More of a minor hiccup really.'

'Penny, what you need is a holiday. I did a quick bit of delving into your horoscope this morning, and what you need, my dear Leo friend, is——'

'Lexy, I'm not in the mood for any of your astrological mumbo-jumbo! What I need is a job and somewhere to live.'

'You need a holiday,' Lexy had repeated imperturbably. 'And fortunately, Aunty Lexy has the ideal one lined up for you.' Lexy Raphael's exotically dark-lashed blue eyes had flashed impatiently with the look Penny had given her. 'You needn't think I'm being in the least altruistic in what I'm about to suggest; you'll be doing me a favour. . . Interested?'

And it had been the most tempting of suggestions: the use of the Raphael villa in the north of Mallorca, and time to lick her wounds before facing the world once more. . .something she sorely needed. But she had turned to the very dear friend who had dipped in and out of her life since their school days, her expression uncertain.

'Lexy, if, as you claim, your flight's booked for tomorrow, a car's awaiting you at Palma airport and the family villa has been opened up to receive you, how is it you're suddenly not going? And for heaven's sake don't tell me it's something to do with your wretched stars, because I'll not believe you!'

'No, it isn't. It's. . .' Lexy had paused, patently stalling. 'I'm needed at the gallery, if you must know.'

'Pull the other one!' had been Penny's retort. The art gallery to which her friend had referred was one privately owned by the Raphael family and one at which Lexy held an exceptionally vague position—her work there had never been known to interfere with her play, which she tended to take very seriously.

'A certain Peter Langton has appeared on the scene,' Lexy had muttered, an expression Penny had found difficulty in interpreting flitting across her face. 'But not to worry, I'll be joining you within a few days—a week at the most—by which time your spirits should be recovered enough for us to live it up a bit.'

A smile filled with affection curved Penny's mouth as she remembered. Could this mysterious Peter Langton be the man to dispel the stunningly beautiful Lexy's cynical conviction that it was her wealth, rather than her looks and personality, that men found so attractive?

The smile died on her lips as a swift surge of pain and outraged indignation welled in her at the memory of Rupert's treachery. . . He had obviously lied when he'd said he loved and wanted to marry her, yet she certainly possessed no fortune that might have led her to suspect the extravagance of his declarations.

'To hell with Rupert—and all men, for that matter,' she muttered savagely to herself as she rounded the last curve of the long drive before bringing the car to a halt with a puzzled frown behind a white and gleamingly expensive-looking convertible car, parked at a careless angle across the closed doors of a line of garages.

She stepped out of the car, glancing around uncertainly as the still-balmy October air wrapped her in its cocoon. This *had* to be the right place, she reasoned with waning conviction. Vague though Lexy had been, she had insisted that the villa couldn't be missed, even in the dark. She gave another glance towards the badly parked car, her features relaxing back to a softly striking beauty. The car probably belonged to a friend who knew of Lexy's planned stay, but not of its postponement, she decided, collecting her luggage.

She approached the huge dark wood front door, deciding to ring the bell instead of using the keys left for her at the airport. She rang several times before having to resort to using the key, and then she was standing in the cool spaciousness of a marbled hall, awe and amazement in the gasp escaping her.

She deposited her luggage at her feet as the soft, lapping sound of water drew her bedazzled gaze towards an archway several yards ahead of her and beyond to a shrubbed patio.

'Lexy, is that you?'

Penny spun round, glancing in confusion from one to the other of the several arches to the left and the right of her, and with no idea from which that deep, echoing sound of a man's voice had emanated.

'Was it my imagination, or did you ring the doorbell just now? I was in the shower. . . Who the hell are *you*?'

The body to which that voice belonged appeared in an archway to the left of her, glistening and naked save for the small towel slung precariously low on lean, muscled hips. It was a darkly tanned and altogether magnificent body, but it was the shock of its unexpected appearance rather than any sense of appreciation that left Penny floundering for words.

'I asked who you were,' repeated the man, now padding towards her on bare feet, with an almost menacing air.

'Good heavens, you must be Lexy's brother!' croaked Penny inanely as the shadows created by the arch fell away to reveal a face with enough of Lexy Raphael's familiar looks in it to be comforting, despite its aggressively masculine and almost startling handsomeness.

'It's *your* identity, not mine, that's in question,' stated the man, halting so close to her that the damp fragrance of his glistening body seemed to wrap itself around her.

'I'm sorry!' exclaimed Penny, making a concerted

effort to collect her scattered wits. 'I'm Penny Elliot—Lexy and I were at school together.'

Amusement glinted in the blue of those familiarly exotic, dark-lashed blue eyes as he returned the shake of the hand Penny had reflexively held out to him.

'Dominic Raphael,' he murmured with a small, mocking bow. 'As you so rightly deduced.' He glanced towards the door. 'Where's Lexy got to?'

'She won't be here for another few days,' responded Penny, her heart sinking on catching the expression of undisguised annoyance on Dominic Raphael's handsome features as he swung round to face her once more.

'Why not? She was due tonight!' he exclaimed, making no attempt to hide his irritation.

'Yes, I know, but. . . Look, I really am sorry—my turning up here instead of Lexy has obviously put you out,' stammered Penny, torn between wishing the ground would open up and swallow her and an overwhelming desire to throttle her infuriating friend for having so thoughtlessly placed her in this embarrassing position. 'I honestly didn't realise there would be anyone else here,' she added, hot colour staining her cheeks as she returned to where she had deposited her luggage by the front door.

'We'd better find you a room.'

'No. . . I'm sure there are still hotels open——'

'I can't see any possible reason why you should feel the need to go racing off to find a hotel—this place isn't exactly cramped,' pointed out Dominic Raphael coolly.

'No, but. . .' Penny broke off with an awkward shrug.

'Don't tell me you're worried about staying here unchaperoned?' he drawled softly, laughter in his eyes.

Penny flashed him a withering look, but said nothing.

The one exception to Lexy's uncompromising silence regarding her family had been the brother almost eight years her senior, whom she plainly adored—though at times with reservations.

'I warned them,' Lexy had fretted guiltily, when two female acquaintances of hers had had their hearts well and truly battered at the cavalier hands of her brother. 'Dominic's gorgeous and I love him to bits, but he's a typical Libran charmer and I wouldn't wish it on my worst enemy to fall in love with him—not till his playboy days are behind him, anyway.'

Charm? wondered Penny dismissively as a pair of openly mocking blue eyes caught and held hers in challenge. Looks he admittedly possessed in abundance, but his charm was something on which she intended reserving judgement.

'Lexy would never forgive me if I frightened off one of her old school chums,' he murmured, adroitly managing to awake in Penny an image of herself as a plump, hockey-stick-toting twelve-year-old. 'And, if it's any consolation, she couldn't have warned you of my presence here because she wasn't warned of it—I only arrived a couple of hours ago.'

'But that doesn't alter the fact that you weren't expecting to share this place with a complete stranger,' muttered Penny, discomfiture mingling with a prickle of animosity.

He flashed her a disconcertingly wicked grin as he picked up one of her cases, holding the precariously draped towel in place with his free hand.

'I was going to suggest you had Lexy's room—I normally like to get to know a woman before she shares my bed. . .though I'll happily make an exception in your case.'

A rueful grin creeping to her lips very much despite herself, Penny made a mental note to keep in mind that it would be foolish in the extreme ever to judge this man by the sister whose disarming grin he had just replicated.

'There's no need for you to go to the trouble of making any exceptions on my behalf,' she told him with false sweetness, picking up the second case. 'Lexy's room will be fine.'

She followed his tall, broad-shouldered figure through the confusing maze of marbled halls, and found herself making idle mental comparisons between his physique and that of Rupert. . . Dominic Raphael won hands down, he was nigh on perfect. And the graceful, almost arrogant self-assurance with which that magnificent body prowled these marble halls left her in little doubt that its owner was all too aware of its masculine perfection.

'Here we are,' he announced, flinging open a door and standing aside as Penny entered a room she could only describe as palatial.

Her eyes widened at first with disbelief as she gazed around the sparsely yet exquisitely furnished room, then in alarm as they alighted on the huge canopied bed in its centre.

'This. . .' she cleared her throat, colour rushing to her cheeks '. . .this *is* Lexy's room, isn't it?'

'Well, it certainly isn't mine, if that's what's bothering you,' he drawled, those mocking eyes of his flickering over her face as he followed her into the room and settling disconcertingly in the region of her right shoulder, almost as though unable to drag themselves away from the thick mass of dark blonde hair they encountered there.

'They say gentlemen prefer blondes, don't they?' he murmured, his eyes remaining on her as though mesmerised while he set down her case. 'But then, as you've no doubt been warned, I'm no gentleman.'

He turned and began walking away from her. 'The door on the left leads to the bathroom and the one on the right to the dressing-room.' He paused as he reached the door. 'There's a cold buffet set out for us in the dining-room—you'd better give me a shout when you're ready to eat, as you'll never find it on your own.' The door was just closing behind him, when he added, 'And try not to take all night, will you? It's late, and I'm hungry.'

There was a sharp glint of anger in Penny's wide-spaced blue eyes as she heard the door close behind him; those last words had managed to sound ominously close to being an order.

'Libran charm—my foot!' she exclaimed aloud, and began unpacking at her leisure.

It was over an hour later when Penny came across him standing, lost in thought, beside a swimming-pool in one of the fascinating inner courtyards around which the villa was built.

He was now dressed—an impeccable cut to his dark, close-fitting trousers and the unmistakable weight of silk to the warm cream of his shirt. His hair was a shade or two darker than Lexy's, observed Penny— almost black, yet with that same familiar tousled hint of curl in it that drove Lexy to distraction whenever she wanted to give an appearance of sleek sophistication.

She watched as he raised a glass to his lips and found herself wondering what her reaction to him might have been under different circumstances. She probably would have fallen head over heels in love with him just as others were alleged to have done, she answered herself morosely; so it was probably just as well Rupert had already done all the damage ever likely to be done

to her heart. . . How could he have deceived her like
that, and with Linda of all people?

She closed her eyes momentarily against the sudden
threat of tears. Lexy always claimed that people born
under the sign of Leo had an abundance of self-
confidence. . .which only went to show how wrong
Lexy's astrological statements could be—this particular
Leo had no shred of confidence left in her!

'There you are.'

Penny jumped as that soft voice drawled its way into
her unhappy thoughts.

'Yes, here I am,' she muttered, struggling to regain
her composure and promising herself that from now on
Rupert was banished from her thoughts.

He turned and faced her fully, his eyes making their
leisurely progress from the ponytail into which she had
tied her still-damp hair and down the length of the
navy T-shirt dress skimming in soft hint over the curves
of her slim body.

'You really shouldn't have rushed like that,' he
murmured drily, pointedly glancing down at the gold
watch nestling among the dark hairs at his wrist.

'I looked for the dining-room, but didn't come across
it,' said Penny, content to ignore his barbed remark
because of the positive boost her ego had experienced
at the sight of the unmistakable gleam of appreciation
she had detected in his eyes in the instant before he
had lowered them to his watch. 'Have you eaten?' she
added.

'No,' he replied, finishing his drink, then strolling to
her side. 'I do have the odd gentlemanly trait or two in
me. . .though, to be completely honest, I don't much
care for eating on my own.' There was the ghost of a
self-deprecating smile on his lips as he gave her a small
bow and offered her his arm.

Penny gave a soft chuckle as she took his arm and

followed his lead, her spirits suddenly lifting. She could think of no better medicine for an ego as battered as hers than a spot of gentle flirtation with a handsome stranger. And if there was comfort to be had from a broken heart, it had to be that no stranger—however handsome—could inflict any further damage on it.

'All of a sudden, I'm starving,' she announced.

'I feel I should warn you of one of the several advantages in not being a gentleman,' murmured Dominic, gazing down at her with a completely straight face. 'I'll have no qualms about fighting you for the tastiest morsels—I'm ravenous.'

Penny's laughter caught in her throat as he led her into what she would have been more inclined to call a banqueting hall rather than merely a dining-room.

'You know, Lexy's typically understated references to this place had me conjuring up mental pictures of something on the lines of a couple of bedrooms, cramped living quarters and a few primitive washing facilities—the outer walls being white was the only thing I got right.'

His reply was a short laugh, one Penny found disconcertingly without humour. Then he made his way to the top of the long table, dark and huge and polished to a mirror finish, where napkin-covered bowls of food were laid out.

'One thing can be said of my grandfather—he appreciated things on a grand scale. Not that this place was ever his. . . But his taste, of course, was another matter altogether.'

The chilling venom with which he had uttered those words made Penny's skin prickle unpleasantly.

'Help yourself,' he suggested, his tone reverting once more to normal as he handed Penny a plate.

'What little I've seen of this place shows exquisite taste,' she stated quietly, unable to believe his remark could have intended criticism of these beautiful surroundings.

'Thank you—I had it completely refurbished a few months ago.'

Something in his tone brought Penny's eyes to his face. She lowered them quickly, wondering what on earth could have brought that grim, almost angry set to his features.

She made to help herself to some prawns from the huge bowl before her, halting in mid-action.

'Is it something I inadvertently said?' she asked.

'Is *what* something you inadvertently said?' he parried uncooperatively, the eyes meeting and holding hers now so coldly challenging that she was almost convinced she must have imagined the gleam of appreciation warming them scant minutes ago.

'For heaven's sake!' she exclaimed, her patience snapping. 'All I did was make a few comments about this place, and. . .and. . .' She broke off in exasperation, returning her still-empty plate to the table.

'And it happened to remind me of my grandfather,' he stated, as though clarifying everything beyond further question.

'So?' exploded Penny impatiently as he began sampling the food straight from the bowls with his fingers.

'So—if you're the great friend of my sister's you claim to be, I'm surprised you need ask,' he muttered with his mouth full.

'What do you mean *if* I'm the friend of Lexy's I *claim* to be?' she demanded aghast, the unnerving thought suddenly occurring to her that she was alone in the middle of nowhere with a man who was beginning to sound more than a little strange.

'Surely Lexy has mentioned our grandfather to you,' he remarked, with a calmness Penny didn't find in the least reassuring.

'No, she didn't! In fact, you're the only member of her family I've ever known her talk about.'

'No doubt to warn you what a bad boy her big brother was,' he drawled.

'Actually, it was to make it plain how much she loved you and looked up to you,' retorted Penny, stung by his inexplicable change of mood. 'Mind you, we were only twelve then—word of your appalling attitude to women didn't come out till years later.'

Penny felt a twinge of satisfaction as Dominic stood for a while in complete silence, gazing down at the food before them in frowning concentration; at least she had made it quite clear that she could give as good as she got.

'Perhaps if we just took the bowl of prawns and some salad out on to the patio—it would be simpler,' he stated. 'Here, take this,' he added, shoving the bowl containing the prawns into her hands and picking up another himself.

For once in her life completely at a loss for words, Penny dazedly followed him through one of the arched doorways and on to a patio with dazzlingly white-painted wood chairs and a large round table.

'I suppose it could be said that you've just shattered a long-held illusion of mine,' he muttered, drawing out a chair for her. 'Hang on a moment,' he added, disappearing only to return second later with a tray laden with a bottle of wine, two glasses, cutlery and napkins and a dish filled with mayonnaise which exuded the pungent aroma of garlic.

In silence, Penny accepted the napkin and cutlery he handed her, the terrible suspicion entering her head that Lexy's inordinate reluctance to discuss her family might just have something to do with a streak of insanity running through it.

'How you behave towards women is your own affair,'

she declared, her pride swept aside by a surfacing streak of self-preservation warning her that she should placate rather than antagonise him. 'I really had no right to make the comment I did—and I certainly had no intention of shattering your illusions.'

She wondered if perhaps she had overdone it when he gave her a slightly alarmed look.

'You *are* the Penny who was at secondary school with Lexy, aren't you—one of the quartet?' he demanded.

Penny nodded, not trusting herself to speak, yet taking a tiny measure of comfort from his reference to the quartet.

'Lexy was expelled from two schools before that one—did you know?'

Again Penny nodded.

'You can't imagine how relieved I was when she seemed to settle down at that third school, especially when she began talking about the three close friends she'd made.'

'The quartet,' murmured Penny, relaxing a little at the realisation that his hitherto rambling words appeared to be leading somewhere. She helped herself to some prawns, watching as his slim fingers deftly shelled several on his plate, and waiting for him to continue.

'Until she met you three I was the only friend she had. As you can imagine, a man of twenty is hardly the ideal confidant for a twelve-year-old girl. . . The illusion you've just shattered is that for all those years I believed she was confiding in her three friends.'

Her eyes wide with shock, Penny shook her head. 'But your parents. . . Surely she could confide in your mother?'

'Both our parents, together with our paternal grandparents, were killed in a plane crash when Lexy was still a baby. I thought girls of that age told their friends everything; didn't the rest of you find it odd her not even mentioning her parents?'

Penny shook her head, an aching sadness filling her. 'It's not that we didn't find it odd. . . There were so many girls around from wealthy yet disastrously unstable backgrounds,' she told him unhappily. 'All three of us realised pretty quickly that family was a taboo subject as far as Lexy was concerned, and we accepted it as such. . . Not that Sarah ever really spoke of her family either, and Erica's parents——' She broke off, her teeth biting sharply against her lower lip.

'Erica's parents?' he probed.

'They had been divorced so often, Erica claimed to have lost count of how many step-parents she had had.'

She gave a start of surprise as he reached over and patted her lightly on the hand.

'Sorry,' he muttered. 'Erica was the one who died a few years ago, wasn't she?'

Penny nodded, unable to speak for the pain she knew would always haunt the remaining three of that childhood quartet.

'And you, Penny, what's your background?' he asked, his deliberate alteration of the course of their conversation leaving her none the wiser as to how much he really knew of the details of Erica's tragic death.

'It's pretty straightforward. The only reason I was sent to that particular school was because my father's a diplomat and he was posted to the back of beyond just before I was twelve.'

'And where are your parents now?'

'Brazil—so naturally I don't see much of them.'

'You should try the mayonnaise with those prawns,' he suggested, with a smile so utterly charming that she had difficulty believing she had earlier judged him to be completely without charm. 'It's very good. . . If you like garlic, that is.'

She tried the mayonnaise and pronounced it delicious.

'And the wine—you haven't tasted that either.'

She took a dutiful sip from her glass and found even her untutored palate suspecting that this must be an exceptionally high quality wine.

'It's fantastic,' she enthused. 'Is it local?'

He gave a small laugh as he shook his head. 'A remark guaranteed to have my grandfather turning in his grave,' he murmured. 'I feel obliged to qualify my remark about his taste—he had an exceptional nose for wine. What you are now sampling is part of a truly magnificent cellar.'

'Did your maternal grandparents bring you both up?' she asked.

'Just the grandfather—he was a widower,' he replied, the grimly closed look returning to his face.

Penny watched in awkward silence as he studiously returned his attention to shelling prawns, an action telling her more plainly than any words that the subject, which he himself had re-opened, was once more closed.

'What do you do for a living?' she eventually asked, responding more to a need to fill the uncomfortably lengthening silence between them than to any particular interest, yet realising the instant the words were out that it was hardly the most apt of questions to be putting to a man probably worth millions.

His eyes flickered towards hers, a hint of something like amusement in them.

'Nothing—I'm a playboy. Didn't you know?' he drawled. 'And since my grandfather died six months ago and his entire business empire passed to me, I have an ever bigger and better toy to play with.' He leaned over and refilled both their glasses, a cold smile on his lips. 'I seem to have shocked you, Penny—though I can't for the life of me think why.'

Penny picked up her glass and almost drained it in an attempt to recover her wits.

'Why on earth should I be shocked?' she asked, shocked to the core not only by the casual malevolence with which he could dismiss a grandfather so recently dead, but also by the realisation that six months ago she had been seeing Lexy more frequently than usual and could, in retrospect, remember no hint of anything resembling grief in her friend at that time.

'Why indeed—yet you obviously are. Haven't you come across a self-confessed playboy before?'

Penny looked at him, plainly having difficulty in believing her ears. 'You know perfectly well it's nothing to do with that! It's your attitude towards your grandfather!' she exclaimed, belying completely her claimed lack of shock.

'What about my attitude towards my grandfather?' he enquired, managing to sound genuinely intrigued.

'Well, he. . . I mean, most people would at least be upset at losing a grandfather—especially one who had also been surrogate mother and father to them.'

'Surrogate mother and father,' he repeated, chuckling reflectively. 'Yes, I dare say you're right—most people would. More wine?'

Penny's nod was absent-minded. Though she still felt residual shock at his callous attitude, she was at the same time realising how completely and irrationally subjective her own reaction was. She took several more gulps of the wine—it really was very good—while trying to sort out her thoughts.

'I admit I was a little shocked. . . And I had absolutely no right to be,' she apologised a little disjointedly. 'After all, I know nothing whatever about your relationship with your grandfather. . . He could have been a complete ogre, for all I know.'

'You're beginning to sound as though you knew him intimately,' he murmured wryly. 'But your spontaneous reaction intrigues me; do you hold that blood ties automatically engender respect—love, even?'

'No, I. . .' Penny found herself once again resorting to draining her wine glass in order to give herself time to think. 'To be honest,' she eventually stated, 'I've had rather a long day.' A perfectly honest statement, she told herself. 'And I'm so tired I can hardly think straight.' She detected no honesty at all in that last statement because tiredness had little or nothing to do with her inability to think coherently.

'How inconsiderate of me,' Dominic replied, rising instantly. 'I'll show you the way back to your room— unless you'd prefer a little more to eat first.'

Penny shook her head, rising also. 'No, that was delicious, thanks.'

She found herself wishing she hadn't shaken her head, then realising exactly how little she had had to eat all day as three, possibly even four glasses of wine started wreaking their merry havoc throughout her senses.

'Perhaps we could finish this interesting conversation tomorrow,' he startled her by saying as he led her back through the dining-room and into that confusing maze of halls.

She glanced up at him, wondering if he was being sarcastic, and found his expression as urbane as his words had sounded. Well, one thing was for sure, she decided dazedly, her unexpected companion wasn't exactly what could be described as an open book— most of the time she hadn't the remotest idea what was going on in his head.

'Are you quite sure you've had enough to eat?' he

asked suddenly, catching her by the elbow as her steps faltered slightly.

'Perfectly, thank you,' replied Penny, her words lilting with the delightful wooziness she was feeling. 'Oh, heavens!' she exclaimed, suddenly stopping short. 'We didn't clear away the things. . . There's all that food left out——'

'Don't worry about it, I'll see to it,' he cut in, his grasp firm on her elbow. 'You need your sleep—you're almost reeling with tiredness,' he added with a soft chuckle.

'You mean from all that wine!' retorted Penny with total candour—she actually *was* reeling! 'You know, apart from those delicious prawns, the only other thing I've had to eat today was a slice of toast early this morning.'

'Well, at least you'll have no problems sleeping in a strange bed,' he chuckled, releasing her arm and opening the door to her room. 'And it's probably way past your bedtime anyway.'

'What time is it?' she asked, glancing down at her wrist. 'I didn't change my watch.'

'Seven minutes to one, I'm afraid,' he replied, then gave another of those soft chuckles she was beginning to find rather attractive—though this one, she noticed, contained a hint of disbelief in it. 'In fact, fifty-three minutes into my thirty-first birthday. . . It is the tenth today, isn't it?'

'It is!' exclaimed Penny delightedly. She loved birthdays, and the very idea of someone actually forgetting his own birthday—even if for only fifty-three minutes— amazed her. 'Happy birthday! If you like, I'll bake you a birthday cake tomorrow. . . Well, today, actually.'

'I think we'd better wait and see how you feel in the morning,' he advised, his eyes twinkling down into hers with open amusement. 'But you might as well give the birthday boy his customary kiss now—in case you're feeling too rough to oblige in the morning.'

'What custom is this?' she asked, laughter bubbling in her voice as he lowered his head to accommodate her, closing his eyes and offering her his lips.

'A local one—I think,' he muttered, through still-posed lips.

'Oh, well, when in Rome. . .' giggled Penny, placing her hands on his shoulders. 'Are you ready?'

'Of course I'm damned well ready—I'm beginning to get a crick in my neck!'

'OK. Happy birthday.'

Having decided that a peck on the cheek was all that could be reasonably required of her—after all, birthday or not, the man was a virtual stranger—Penny was thrown to find her lips against a mouth, instead of the cheek at which she had aimed. And it was a mouth that no longer held any trace of its former puckered innocence; it was one taking its welcome unquestioningly for granted, parting her lips with practised command while his arms wound confidently around her body. And Penny's own arms moved, as though of their own volition, to twine and cling around his neck, her lips spontaneously giving the welcome demanded of them as her body became invaded by a multitude of wild sensations hitherto unknown to it.

'Not merely a happy birthday,' he murmured huskily, when at last obliged to come up for air. 'But a most unexpectedly happy one indeed.'

Drugged by the delightful sensations coursing through her, Penny dispensed with words altogether, impatiently drawing his mouth back to hers. . . She had never experienced anything remotely like this before and was only too eager to prolong the experience.

It was only when his tightening arms lifted her almost off her feet that Penny became aware he had manoeuvred them both through the door and into her room. And it was then, too, that a vague awareness of the total lack of any inhibition she was displaying began dawning on her.

'What a delightful unexpected birthday present you've turned out to be,' he whispered, his hands sliding purposefully over her body.

'Dominic!' she shrieked, full awareness engulfing her like an avalanche even as her body leapt in frantic excitement to his touch. 'Look, I'm sorry. . . I really am!' Terrifying images of what could happen to women who had behaved with the mindless stupidity she had just displayed were flashing through her mind. 'I've obviously had far much more to drink than I'd realised. . . I honestly don't usually behave in the least like this!' she babbled frantically.

'How disappointing!' he grinned, a trifle breathless as he released her. 'I was really rather enjoying it all.'

'I don't know what happened,' she gulped, disconcerted to find the delightful sensations still rioting on unabated within her. 'I mean. . . I was going to kiss your cheek.'

'I much preferred it the way it turned out,' he murmured, the sultry, dangerously suggestive darkness in his eyes worryingly increasing rather than dampening the tumultuous excitement within her. 'As I'm sure you did.'

'No! I. . . Please!' she croaked incoherently, then watched dazedly as he strolled to the door and blew her a mocking kiss before stepping out and closing it behind him.

Penny stood as though rooted where he had left her. She was probably having a mental breakdown, she decided—a decision she welcomed with a ludicrous sense of relief. The traumas of the past week were finally taking their toll. . . There could be no other explanation for the fact that, when Dominic Raphael had closed the door behind him, there had been part of her silently shrieking out to him to come back.

CHAPTER TWO

'GOOD morning, *señorita*.'

Penny began struggling from the depths of sleep as those words reached her, wincing as the swish of the curtains brought light flooding into the room.

'Señor Raphael says to tell you he will join you for breakfast on the pool terrace whenever you are ready.'

The door had already closed behind the maid uttering those words by the time Penny had struggled upright.

She had a bit of a headache, she thought groggily, as the aroma of coffee drew her attention to the tray the maid had placed unnoticed on the bedside-table. She poured herself a cup, idly wondering if her headache warranted taking an aspirin. Then full wakefulness hit her with a devastating thud.

Headache? She should be in the throes of an almighty hangover, she berated herself as horror and humiliation swept over her. Harshly dismissing her conclusion of the night before—that she was in the throes of a mental breakdown—as the product of drunken reasoning, she masochistically began poring over every conceivable detail of her behaviour up to the moment Dominic Raphael had finally left her room.

'It wasn't me!' she groaned aloud, slumping back against the pillows in weak disbelief and almost spilling her coffee. Admittedly she rarely drank more than a couple of glasses of wine with a meal; and all right, so she had had more than her usual quota—and on an empty stomach—but it should never have had that appallingly libidinous effect on her!

Frowning, and with her mind racing, Penny slowly drank her coffee, and gradually her frown eased and she began laughing weakly.

If only Rupert had been a fly on the wall last night! She pulled a face. The truth was that Rupert would never have believed what he was seeing, she admitted glumly. In fact, he would have had no difficulty whatsoever in concluding that the woman responding to Dominic Raphael's kisses with such unbridled enthusiasm could only have been her double.

She finished her coffee, still lost in thought as she poured herself another.

Though Rupert had never actually come right out with it and accused her of being frigid, it was a matter that had always loomed silent and unresolved between them.

She closed her eyes, her features tightening with misery. Which was why his unfaithfulness hadn't altogether surprised her, she reluctantly admitted—the first time she had done so. It was that it was her flatmate with whom he had become involved that hurt so deeply, she now also had to admit.

Perhaps had Rupert tried plying her with drink to loosen her inhibitions things might have turned out differently.

She took several sips from the cup before accepting the niggling thought now chasing through her mind, and once she had accepted it she realised that she could safely bet every penny she possessed that no amount of booze would ever have resulted in her responding to Rupert as she had to a complete stranger last night.

Yet it was Rupert she loved, she reminded herself miserably, finishing her coffee in one gulp. And Rupert who had badgered her to marry him despite the unresolved question of her lack of appreciable physical response to him.

With a sigh she returned the cup to the tray and only then noticed the large sheet of paper, folded several times, behind the coffee-pot. She removed it and opened it out before her on the bed, smiling involuntarily to see it was the plans of the villa, then laughing aloud at the cryptic note scrawled across the top of the sheet in a firm masculine hand.

'Just in case you get lost—strategic areas marked by asterisks.' The signature, a bold 'D', was followed by the postscript, 'How's the head?'

Her initial amusement suddenly faltering, Penny gave a soft groan of frustration as she felt the colour rush to her cheeks; deep down she had been banking on his having sufficient tact not to refer to her drunken behaviour of the previous night.

And to think that she had actually contemplated a little light flirtation with this man, she reflected uncomfortably as she dressed after her quick shower. . .had actually regarded it as a possible means of boosting her deflated ego!

She dawdled before the mirror, running a comb through the shining thickness of her hair and dithering about whether to put it up or not. She decided to leave it as it was, her attention now flitting to the faded blue of the shirt-dress, belted neatly at her trim waist. She was hardly a picture of sophistication, she mused with dissatisfaction, but then she had come here expecting to laze around doing nothing and had packed accordingly. She froze, suddenly acutely conscious of her train of thought. Even dolled up to the nines, it would take a lot more than she had to hold the attention of a self-confessed playboy like Dominic Raphael for more than a few brief moments. . .and her ego had already suffered more than enough damage as it was!

Scowling, and futilely wishing she had never listened to Lexy in the first place, she grabbed the plans and studied them, a smile once again creeping of its own volition to her lips as she found her boldly asterisked room and the trail of arrows leading from there to the terrace.

'You found it,' Dominic observed, glancing up from something he was writing when she eventually joined him.

'Yes—thanks for the plans,' she replied, appalled by the fact that her stomach had lurched into a series of disruptive somersaults the instant she had spotted him.

There was definitely something wrong with her, she decided apprehensively, taking a seat while he placed what he had been writing on a spare chair.

'Just some toast will be fine, thanks. . . *Gracias*,' she said in response to the maid appearing at her side and asking what she would like.

'Do you speak Spanish?' enquired Dominic.

She shook her head. 'That was virtually a third of my entire vocabulary.' While she spoke she was attempting to take calm stock of the man before her, and her decidedly uncalm reaction to him. Yes, he *was* one of the most physically attractive men she had ever clapped eyes on, but that explained nothing—she just wasn't the type given to swooning over men, no matter what their looks.

'Coffee?' he enquired.

'Thank you.' Perhaps her recent ghastly experiences had affected her far more severely than she was aware. . .

'I'll give you a peseta for them.'

'I beg your pardon?' she exclaimed, starting slightly.

'I offered you a peseta for them—those deeply

engrossing thoughts of yours,' he explained with a relaxed smile.

'Sorry,' she muttered, and immediately attempted to mask her paralysing embarrassment by offering unnecessarily profuse thanks to the maid arriving with a mound of toast. 'I seem to be having difficulty adjusting to being here—it's probably because I came very much on the spur of the moment.'

'Probably. I take it you don't work,' he stated.

She glanced across at him, her look strained and uncertain.

'Not many jobs allow people to take off on spur-of-the-moment holidays,' he explained, a slight edge to his tone.

'Oh, I see,' exclaimed Penny, praying she would manage to snap out of this ridiculous state she was in before making an utter fool of herself. 'No. . . I don't work.' Not exactly the truth, but at least it would spare her from tortuous explanation.

'Ah—a playgirl,' he murmured, the slight narrowing of his eyes giving Penny the distinct impression she was being comprehensively assessed.

'No, I—I do quite a bit of charity work.' She hastily began buttering herself a slice of toast in an attempt to mask her own astonishment at the ease with which she had come out with that ridiculous lie—and also to dispel the sound of Lexy's incredulous laughter ringing loudly in her ears.

'What sort of charity work?' he asked, again the faintest of edges to his tone.

'Oh—this and that,' muttered Penny vaguely, and in her distracted annoyance with herself for having started all this, she accidently crammed almost half a slice of toast into her mouth and choked.

'Well, perhaps there will be an opportunity for you to continue your good work here. I need a female brain to pick—I'd hoped it would be Lexy's, but I'm sure yours will do just as well,' he stated, watching, with no offer of assistance, as she struggled for breath.

'I'll gladly help, if I can,' croaked Penny rashly, gulping down a full glass of orange juice for relief.

'It's concerning the hotel.' He paused, frowning. 'Lexy did happen to mention we own an hotel here, didn't she?'

Penny shook her head, her lungs recovered, but noting fatalistically that her feelings of dazed bewilderment were beginning to take on a depressingly settled permanency.

'Hell, she'd hardly have been breaking any of her self-imposed taboos mentioning that,' he muttered impatiently, as though to himself. 'The fact is, we do own an hotel here—unfortunately now kitsch beyond belief—and about which I intend doing something.' He broke off, glancing down at his watch. 'I'm afraid I'll have to be off—I'm picking my secretary up from the airport just after ten, and we'll be going straight to the hotel.' He rose, picking up his coffee-cup and draining it. 'Juana will show you where everything is in the kitchen; see you later.'

She watched as he strode off, her face depicting forlorn bewilderment. He turned, grinning as he caught her look.

'My birthday cake—you offered to bake me one last night, remember? Or was that the wine talking?'

Much more of this and she would be a complete nervous wreck, she thought frustratedly, slumping back against her chair while his parting, softly mocking laughter lingered on in her ears.

Half the time she hadn't the faintest idea what he was talking about, she fumed; and he had a habit of putting off explaining himself just long enough for her to be convinced he was insane. And he had sat there without so much as a flicker of concern while she could have been choking to death for all he cared. As for his impatience with Lexy's penchant for secrecy—it was laughable; he was scarcely any more forthcoming than she was. And another thing; since when did a playboy have a secretary?

She leaned back, closing her eyes as the gentle warmth of the sun caressed her face. With a bit of luck he wouldn't be staying long and she would be able to have a few days of peace on her own before Lexy arrived.

'The telephone for you, *señorita*,' announced the maid, approaching her and carrying a portable phone.

'Penny, it's Lexy——'

'Lexy, boy, do I have a bone to——'

'Penny, is Dominic there?'

'No—he's gone to Palma to——'

'But he *has* arrived!' exlaimed Lexy.

'Yes. And today's his——'

'His birthday, yes. Listen, Penny, you haven't mentioned Peter Langton's name to him, have you?'

'No. Lexy——'

'Thank heavens for that!'

'Lexy, is there any likelihood of my ever being allowed to finish a sentence in this conversation?' demanded Penny.

'Sorry, Penny, It's just that. . . Penny, you definitely haven't mentioned Peter Langton's name to him?'

'Lexy! Why all this panic?' asked Penny exasperatedly. 'Who exactly is this Peter Langton, anyway?'

'No one terribly important,' replied Lexy, her tone striving unsuccessfully for dismissiveness. 'It's just that, well. . . Dominic and he don't get on too well—in fact, you could say Dominic loathes him. . . It'll cause the most awful rumpus if you so much as mention his name.'

'I take it you don't share Dominic's views on him,' chuckled Penny, intrigued to hear her usually eloquent friend for once struggling for words.

'I'll explain when I see you—I'll be with you a week tomorrow,' said Lexy, plainly hedging.

Penny frowned in disbelief. Though Lexy maintained an implacable silence where her family was concerned, she tended to discuss the men in her life with a sometimes startling candour. . . This Peter Langton was obviously *very* special!

'So tell me, Penny, how are you getting on with my delectable brother?'

'You've changed your tune, haven't you?' exclaimed Penny. 'I thought your beloved brother was the one man you felt obliged to protect all women from. You were hopping mad over the way he treated——'

'Yes, I know,' butted in Lexy, and immediately apologised abjectly for having done so. 'But that was a few years ago and anyway, you're not likely to disgrace yourself by falling for him. So tell me, how are the two of you getting on?'

'Frankly, I find him completely baffling—worse even than you at your very worst, if that's possible.'

Lexy gave a chuckle of delight. 'I know,' she sympathised. 'Librans have a knack of driving you to distraction at times, but Dominic has all the charm and personality you could ever hope to find in one. Mind you, he has a temper that more than balances all that, when he loses it—which isn't often——'

'Lexy, spare me the astrological analysis,' groaned Penny. 'How did you discover he was here, anyway?'

'I rang his Paris office to wish him happy birthday—that's how.'

'His office?' Penny exlaimed. 'And he's just gone to Palma to pick up his secretary; I thought he was supposed to be a dedicated playboy. . . Or is this apparent dichotomy something peculiar to all Librans?'

'Penelope, my love, you're beginning to sound inordinately interested in my big, bad, beautiful brother,' teased Lexy. 'I think I'll have to do a bit of swotting up on Leos and Librans. . .'

'Lexy, are you still there?' asked Penny, as the line suddenly went silent.

'Sorry, Penny,' came Lexy's oddly strained voice. 'I have to go. Wish Dominic a happy birthday from me— see you next week.'

'Lexy, could you. . .?' She broke off as she heard the phone click. Lexy had hung up.

Dusk had fallen by the time Dominic returned, and Penny's slowly acquired feeling of well-being remained intact when her stomach mercifully showed no inclination to repeat its acrobatics of the morning at this, her second sight of him.

She had spent a delightfully lazy day, familiarising herself with her beautiful surroundings, swimming, and being plied on and off with delicious titbits by the cheerfully motherly Juana.

'Sorry to have left you on your own for so long,' apologised Dominic, joining her by the softly splashing fountain in one of the smaller courtyards. 'Would you like a drink?'

'Oh, I'd love——' She broke off, colouring furiously. 'No, thanks.'

'Forget about last night,' he grinned. 'You have to remember you were drinking after a long day's journey and on top of an empty stomach—and I very much doubt if it's empty today, if I know Juana.'

Penny smiled. 'I get the impression she thinks I need fattening up; she really is a fantastic cook.'

'You're speaking to one of her most ardent fans,' he

laughed. 'So—how about a glass of Grandpa's vintage champagne?'

'Well. . .as it's your birthday,' she conceded with a grin.

'That reminds me—where's my cake?'

'If sir would care to follow me,' she murmured, 'I'll lead him to it.'

'You didn't actually bake me one, did you?' he demanded through laughter as she led him towards the dining-room.

'Actually, it's a joint effort,' she admitted, wondering if he would think her unspeakably childish if she were to ask him to close his eyes before entering the room—and deciding he would. 'Juana baked it and I iced it. . . Unfortunately we could only come up with one candle.'

'That's a relief,' he replied. 'I doubt if I'd have the puff to blow out thirty-one in a single blow. . . Penny, it's a work of art!' he enthused as she led him to the table.

'Do you really think so?' she asked, secretly flattered by his reaction. 'I know it looks a bit like snow on a Christmas cake, but I had to do that because the icing refused to go on smoothly.'

'I love it,' he declared uninhibitedly. 'I'll nip off and get the bubbly—then we can sample it.'

Penny felt a warm glow of satisfaction creep over her as he disappeared. He actually was a very nice man, she reflected with a small stab of surprise. It wasn't as though she was discounting his ghastly hobby of breaking women's hearts, which even his adoring sister admitted he did with horrifying ease, it was just that the delightful, almost boyish enthusiasm he had exhibited over the cake indicated a totally different side to him.

'Oh, heck!' she whispered in alarm to herself. 'I

hope I got the proportions right for the icing.' A bad mix had been known to break teeth.

'It's a shame I didn't manage to get back a bit earlier, then Juana could have joined us before she left,' Dominic said on his return.

'She's concocted the most wonderful selection of *tapas* for supper—she says they're your favourite. They look good, but I'm not really sure what they are.'

'Unbelievably delicious titbits—you haven't lived until you've tasted Juana's *tapas*!' he declared, uncorking the champagne. 'Here,' he said, tossing her a box of matches. 'You light the candle while I pour this.'

She lit the candle, giving the icing a surreptitious prod with a finger as she did so; it gave to perfection.

'I forgot to tell you—Lexy rang this morning to wish you a happy birthday. She'll be arriving a week tomorrow.'

'What's keeping her in London?' he asked, handing her a glass.

'Something to do with the gallery, I think,' replied Penny, puzzled and slightly irritated with herself to feel her cheeks colouring.

'No, it's nothing to do with that,' said Dominic. 'I tried getting her there this morning when I had no success at her place—they weren't expecting her and hadn't any idea where she might be.' He broke off with a sudden exclamation. 'I'd better do the necessary with that candle before it starts dripping all over your icing.' He clinked the rim of his glass to hers, wished himself many happy returns, took a gulp of champagne and then a deeply exaggerated breath.

'Don't forget to make a wish,' Penny reminded him through her laughter.

He blew out the candle and turned to her with an altogether wicked grin. 'Would you like to hear my wish?' he murmured teasingly.

'It won't come true if you tell it,' she informed him, a trifle sharply because her stomach had maliciously taken to performing acrobatics once more—not that he had seemed to have heard either her words or their sharpness; he was busy transferring things to a trolly.

'We'll take this lot out on to the patio and have it there,' he announced.

Penny followed him out, remonstrating furiously with her recalcitrant stomach—then realised what she was doing and almost threw up her hands in disbelief.

'Don't I get a second wish when I cut the cake?' he asked, cutting into it.

'Not that I've heard of,' laughed Penny, her spirits reviving a fraction. 'By the way, where's your secretary?' she asked, watching as he served two enormous slices of cake on to plates.

'She's staying in Alcudia—her sister lives there.'

'Is she Spanish?'

'No, French—her sister's married to a Mallorcan doctor.' He handed her a plate, topped up their glasses, and then took a mouthful of cake.

Penny watched in trepidation, her mind filling with what seemed like every word Lexy had ever uttered regarding Librans and their famed finickiness—their allegedly unremitting need for an aesthetic harmony amounting to virtual perfection whether it was in their surroundings, the clothes they wore or the food they ate. And Juana's cake, she reflected gloomily, had been well-nigh perfect until all that icing had been ladled over it.

'Well?' she demanded, when he seemed to have munched for at least a full minute.

He made a sound that was completely unintelligible.

'What did you say?'

His mere repetition of the sound drove her to tasting the cake for herself—she found it absolutely delicious.

'As I said—twice—the best-iced cake I've ever tasted,' he announced ambiguously, and promptly took another mouthful.

Her spirits now almost totally revived, Penny followed suit; he was right, it *was* delicious, icing and all!

'I was wondering,' he stated companionably. 'This spur-of-the-moment flight of yours here; what were you running away from?'

Penny managed to catch her fork before it clattered to the marbled patio slabs.

'Nothing,' she lied through a painfully clenched jaw. Never, she vowed silently, would she ever again allow herself to relax in this nerve-racking man's company! 'Why on earth should I be running away from something?' she asked, striving desperately to mask her inner feelings. 'I was a bit bored and felt like a break.'

'Bored with all your charities?' he murmured with palpable coolness. 'Perhaps you should get yourself a proper job.'

'You're a fine one to talk!' she snapped, her quick temper scattering caution to the winds. 'A self-confessed playboy!'

'You misunderstand me; I wasn't necessarily advocating that you *should* work, simply that it might be a cure for your boredom.'

Penny took another mouthful of cake, furiously cursing her casual lie of the previous evening. She had no one but herself to blame for this—though, for someone as reticent about his own life as he was, he certainly had a nerve prying into hers like this!

'And I didn't say I don't work,' he continued.

'Oh, yes, I forgot—your grandfather left you a business empire to play with,' she retorted.

'There is such a thing as creative play,' he murmured without any apparent rancour. 'And in my creatively playful hands I can assure you the business will go from strength to strength—without my having to lift much more than a finger.'

'Banking on beginner's luck, are you?' she asked unkindly.

'Not in the least. I already have a thriving architectural practice in Paris which I started up from scratch.'

Penny tried hard to mask her astonishment.

'But if you have a perfectly legitimate profession, why on earth do you refer to yourself as a playboy?' she demanded exasperatedly.

'Conditioning, my dear Penelope, conditioning,' he drawled infuriatingly.

Penny flashed him a hostile look. At least Lexy said nothing about her family, unlike this man, who would make engimatic references to it and then get on his high horse when she rose to the bait!

'Why do you and Lexy hate your grandfather so much?' she demanded, anger goading her into calling his bluff.

'What makes you think we hate him?' he stalled, his eyes expressing a hostility that more than matched hers.

'The tone of your voice when you mention anything remotely concerning him,' she replied, refusing to be intimidated. 'And the fact that Lexy has never once so much as mentioned him.'

'It seems Lexy rarely mentions me, yet you don't doubt her love for me,' he countered, his eyes bright with the glitter of granite.

'Oh, forget it!' exclaimed Penny, her patience snapping completely. 'You're quite happy to pry into my life, but not nearly as happy if I try the same with you. . . So let's just drop the subject!'

'How could you possibly accuse me of prying?' he protested, suddenly an exaggerated picture of wide-eyed innocence. 'When I hadn't even got round to

asking you about the man—or men— in your life? I'm
sure a woman as beautiful as you are must be knee-
deep in them.' He flashed her a calculatedly stunning
smile. 'Tell me, Penny, was it a man you came speeding
to my Mallorcan lair to escape from?'

'That's called the third degree, not prying!' she
gasped, laughter bursting from her at his sheer audacity.

'Now, that's much better,' he murmured, his eyes
twinkling. 'And I really must remind you to be more
careful in your treatment of me on my birthday,
because my mother always told me I'd turn into a
grease-spot if I cried on that particular day. . . I'd hate
to discover she was right.'

'You still remember your parents?' asked Penny,
inexplicably surprised.

'Of course I do—I was nine when they died.' The
laughter left his eyes. 'I remember their warmth and
their constant laughter—and above all the absolute
love they personified.' He raised his glass to his lips
and drained it, as though drinking a private toast. 'And
yes, I did hate my grandfather. I hated him for his
coldness, his aversion to laughter, and his total ignor-
ance of the concept of love.'

'Dominic. . . I'm sorry,' she whispered, the savage
bitterness in his words chilling her to the core. 'I should
never have mentioned him.'

'Why not?' he rasped. 'Not mentioning his name
won't erase what he was. . .nor the cheerless, loveless
routine into which he regimented our lives—especially
Lexy's.' He leaned back, his eyes staring sightlessly
into the distance of his terrible memories. 'I had had
nine years of my parents' unstinting love to cushion
me; all Lexy ever had was the memories I used to share
with her. To Lexy, my memories of our parents were
the fairy-tales of her childhood.'

'But what made him like that. . .your grandfather?' asked Penny, tears blurring her eyes.

He gave an angry shrug. 'Some people are born with deformities that aren't immediately apparent. . .perhaps his was the lack of a soul.'

'But he married your grandmother. . .' Her words petered to a perplexed halt.

'And he fathered my mother, the most loving of women,' he concurred woodenly. 'Perhaps he was normal once, but I can only speak for the man I knew—and that man was entirely without soul.'

'But you and Lexy have turned out all right, despite him,' stated Penny, the only words of consolation she could offer.

'Have we?' he questioned with infinite bitterness. 'It seems my sister is incapable of confiding even in her few closest friends, and, as for men, her attitude to them isn't exactly straightforward; she'll go to any lengths rather than risk a close relationship with one.'

Feeling almost as though it were a betrayal of her friend, Penny found herself unable to deny the truth in his words. Lexy always froze men out, whether by claiming they were after her money or subjecting them to what virtually amounted to ridicule by her candid disclosures to her friends.

'But you're right about her feelings towards me,' he continued, his tone almost expressionless. 'Her love for me is such that she closes her eyes to what I really am. No matter how badly I behave, she'll always delve into the stars and come up with one excuse or another for me.'

'But you're not being fair!' exclaimed Penny, leaping to Lexy's defence despite the fact that she was very much in two minds about the subject of astrology. 'You can't deny that Lexy can often tell a person's sign soon after meeting them.'

'You're missing my point,' he said quietly. 'I was querying your statement regarding how Lexy and I had turned out. I was merely pointing out that we both seem compelled to keep the opposite sex at arm's length.'

Penny's eyes widened with incredulity; every scrap of what little she had heard of Dominic, not to mention his attitude the night before, gave total lie to such a claim.

'Perhaps, in the light of last night, I should have phrased that differently,' he murmured. 'Physically, I like women very much closer than arm's length; emotionally, it's another matter. Once the word "love" starts getting bandied about I feel it only fair to disentangle myself.'

'Fair?' enquired Penny, with open scepticism.

'Perhaps you'd care to tell me what you do,' he suggested blandly. 'You're involved with a man whose company you enjoy, but with whom you're neither in love nor likely to be. What do you do when that man starts telling you he loves you, perhaps even starts mentioning marriage and children?'

'I'd tell him the truth,' stated Penny firmly.

'Would you continue the relationship?'

'No. . . It would hardly be fair——'

'Hardly fair if I were to either, wouldn't you agree?'

'Yes, but the difference is that I wouldn't go into a relationship with the attitude that love is something to be avoided like the plague.'

'You go in looking for love, do you?'

'No! I. . .' She had leapt in with both feet as usual, she realised wretchedly, as it now dawned on her that what he referred to as relationships she would call affairs.

'Penny, I don't regard love as something to be avoided like the plague. . .it's just something I've never experienced.' He gave a deep, throaty chuckle. 'Perhaps I'm just a late developer. And who knows? Perhaps by the end of the week I'll be down on my knees, languishing with love for you. . .and you'll be doing what's only fair and thereby giving me a taste of my own medicine.' His eyes caught and held hers in their teasing laughter, while she frantically racked her brains for a witty response. 'It's getting a bit chilly out here,' he announced, as she continued her fruitless search. 'Let's go inside and see what delights Juana has left us.' He rose, casually holding out a hand to her.

Penny hesitated momentarily, then placed her hand in his.

'Tell me, Penny, are you really not looking for love?' he murmured mockingly.

'No, I'm damned well not!' she exclaimed, snatching back her hand.

'So, if I do happen to fall in love with you, I'm in for a really tough time of it.'

'Far rougher than you could possibly imagine,' she replied, regaining her composure with merciful speed—only to have it ruffled once more by amused exasperation as he began staggering towards the house, clutching theatrically at his heart.

The woman who ever managed to awaken love in this man was certainly going to have her hands full, she thought, a chuckle of disbelief escaping her as she followed him indoors.

CHAPTER THREE

'Do YOU mean to tell me that poor girl was on holiday?' gasped Penny, halfway through a late lunch after having taken his secretary to the airport. 'She only had about five days here, and you had her at your beck and call for most of them!'

'Don't exaggerate,' Dominic rebuked lightly, no trace of guilt marring his handsome features. 'Monique knows how I value her opinion.'

Penny gazed across at him in bemused fascination as he resumed eating. She considered she had got to know him quite well during the past few days, but only to the extent of accepting that he was one of the most baffling people she was ever likely to meet.

'I'm surprised you'd feel the need of Monique's opinion, with all those experts you seem to have at your beck and call.' The plumbing specialist from Germany and the glazier from Italy to name but two, she thought, shuddering to think what the final cost of the renovations would be.

'You know what they say about a woman's touch,' he murmured, grinning. 'And flattered though I am that you seem to consider me capable of doing it all single-handed, I have to admit there are times when even a genius of my calibre has to consult the odd expert or three.'

'You make it sound ominously as though you plan razing the place to the ground and starting all over,' she groaned, laughing.

'God forbid!' he exclaimed, his expression pained. 'My intention is to restore it to what it once was. . .and

not simply for old times' sake, either. And for that I
need all the experts money can buy.'

'Why do you say "not simply for old times' sake"?'
Dominic was a highly intelligent man, and self-
possessed often to the point of arrogance. Yet Penny
found herself wondering if there weren't a part of him
capable of clinging to the aestheticism of a half-
forgotten past.

'Take the original entrance to the hotel, for
example,' he suggested. 'There were marbled ramps
running up both sides of the steps leading up to it.'

'Which you plan to restore?'

He nodded. 'Yes, but by restoring the façade of the
building to its original elegance we also just happen to
provide two ramps capable of accommodating wheel-
chairs—a most pertinent consideration in any day and
age, wouldn't you agree?'

'Of course I would—that's fantastic!' she exclaimed.
'But not something many would have thought of.'

'To be honest, I hadn't immediately seen it from that
angle,' he grinned, giving her foot a playful kick
beneath the table as she feigned astonishment at his
admission. 'It was Miguel, the hotel manager, who first
spotted it.'

'Yet Lexy's proved right again,' murmured Penny
teasingly. 'The Libran penchant for looking at things
from every conceivable angle really does pay off.'

'If you say so, though Miguel could be a Martian for
all I know,' he stated, deliberately misunderstanding
her, while at the same time deftly hooking her feet
forward with his own and, with no hint on his face as
to what he was up to, trapping her legs lightly between
his.

'Dominic!' she hissed, colour leaping to her cheeks.

'I must be a masochist—I can't wait for you to start
breaking my heart,' he murmured. 'Besides, I like

seeing you blush.' He then gave his attention to an approaching waiter and ordered coffee, while at the same time exerting the slightest of pressure against her calves with his. 'Would you like anything with your coffee?'

She shook her head, glowering at him. The infuriating thing was that, ever since the night of his birthday, her blushes were a sight he had taken to conjuring up at will by sporadically flying off at a tangent from serious conversation into teasing flirtation. On the one occasion his light flirtation had been on the verge of progressing towards open sexual propositioning, he had made the transition with such delicacy and charm that it had been some time before she had become aware of its having been made.

'For a grown man you can be amazingly childish at times,' she snapped, silently cursing this complete inability of hers to judge when he was about to unleash this side of him on her—one which invariably caught her with her guard down.

'You know, Penny, I sometimes wonder about the men in your life,' he said softly. 'Something tells me they must be an incredibly boring bunch.'

'Why—because they're not childish like you?' she retaliated.

'I can assure you, there's nothing remotely childish in my intentions towards you,' he advised her, completely unruffled. 'I'm beginning to think it was a stroke of fate that brought you here to me. . . I can think of nothing more delightful than rectifying your intriguing ignorances regarding men.'

'You—I can't believe I'm hearing this!' she floundered. 'If you must know, I had to come here to. . .to think over a proposal from the man I happen to love.' She wasn't sure which appalled her more—her ruinously quick temper having launched her into this, her second lie; or that she had only just managed to stop herself childishly adding 'so there!' to her mendacious claim.

'Aha—the truth at last!' he laughed. 'And the mere fact you had to think it over, let alone leave the country to do so, should have told you your answer is no,' he pointed out, with the air of one stating the completely obvious. 'What exactly was he proposing, anyway?'

'Marriage,' she exclaimed indignantly.

'Oh, dear, you really do have problems don't you?' he murmured with patently false sympathy.

'And what exactly is that supposed to mean?'

'You have to admit that you responded to my kisses the other night with a lot more enthusiasm than would be expected in a woman in love—with another man, that is.'

'I was drunk, for heaven's sake!' she almost shrieked.

'Of course you weren't drunk,' he responded dismissively. 'You had a couple of glasses of wine on an empty stomach——'

'Could we just drop this?' she cut in angrily, an unpleasant sense of foreboding warning her that she was going to regret this second lie a great deal more than the first.

'But of course,' he replied, the epitome of cooperation. 'What would you like us to talk about instead?'

She glowered across the table at him. 'Can't we just go?'

'I've just ordered coffee and, being a creature of habit, I'd like my customary couple of cups of it after lunch.'

Creature of habit he most certainly was not, she fumed silently. In fact, he was so completely unpredictable that she was beginning to wonder if he had ever done the same thing twice in his entire life.

'Juana tells me we're in for rain,' he continued sociably.

Penny felt herself tense automatically. The weather was hardly a contentious subject, but she had few doubts that he could turn it into a full-scale debate if he so chose.

'I'm surprised you decided to come here at a time when the weather isn't reliable,' she muttered.

'Why not? I rather like rain,' he replied. 'And anyway, as this is a working holiday, I had no option to come other than when the hotel was closed for the season.'

'Well, Lexy will be here any day now,' she continued, her unspoken 'thank heavens' taken care of by her tone.

'Do I bring out the worst in you, Penny?' Dominic queried softly, his eyes capturing hers in that a way she found impossible to draw free from.

'Yes. . . I'm afraid you do,' she admitted deflatedly, suddenly inordinately conscious of the still-unchanged position of their legs, and desperately willing her cheeks not to burn yet again. 'Dominic, are you really going to run your grandfather's business?' she asked, clumsily changing the subject. 'What about your own business?'

He paused as the waiter brought and served the coffee.

'I've had to run down my workload in Paris, but my partners are prepared to fill in for me as long as is necessary,' he told her. 'You see, my grandfather didn't exactly saddle me with a corner shop. . .it's a world-wide conglomeration.' He paused, the grim remoteness so evident whenever he spoke of his grandfather returning to his face. 'It's far too big a concern for one man to have the powers of veto over decision-making as he had. I'm not denying he had an astute business brain—but he could also be vindictive and divisive when experts, who had every right, questioned the advisability of some of his interferences.'

'And the business suffered?'

'Yes—though with profits so vast it's not something immediately apparent.' He drained his coffee and signalled to a waiter for more. 'In the past six months, since my grandfather's death, I've been working towards placing autonomy where it belongs in the company—that is, in the hands of those paid to do the job and who, in my opinion, do it admirably. Besides,' he added, suddenly freeing her legs, 'all of this extra work interferes with my play.'

'Why do you say it's conditioning that makes you refer to yourself as a playboy?' Penny asked.

'Do I say that?' he demanded, shrugging when she nodded. 'Lexy and I inherited our paternal grand-parents' estate on their death—mainly vineyards in France and Italy, but also the gallery in London and the hotel and villa here. . . My remaining grandfather's trusteeship ran out when I became eighteen, which he didn't like in the least.' Dominic paused, his eyes flickering mockingly towards hers. 'Though his refer-ring to me as a playboy might also have had something to do with the succession of his secretaries I seduced—until he learned his lesson and chose them less nubile.'

'And I suppose your seduction of them had nothing to do with upsetting your grandfather,' she observed tartly.

'Nothing,' he murmured blandly. 'His wrath was merely an added bonus.'

'Why on earth did he leave you everything if he considered you so dissolute?'

'Because the terms of his own inheritance dictated it be left to the nearest blood male—yours truly.'

'But the hotel and the villa—if they were already

yours in the first place, why have you waited until now to alter them?' she asked, puzzled.

'I told you—he was my trustee. He couldn't meddle in the vineyards, because of the terms of Grandpa Raphael's will, so to compensate—he was a compulsive meddler—he gave his appalling taste free rein in the hotel and villa. . . God, the only thing that appealed to him about the villa was its size!'

Penny felt herself shiver inwardly as she saw the depths of the loathing simmering beneath that urbane surface.

'You see, I could remember both before he had left his ugly stamp on them. . . Sometimes, as a child, I used to feel physically sick to see how he had desecrated them. But the good memories always brought me back here—yes, at eighteen I *could* have rectified it, but I had the threat of being barred from seeing Lexy hanging over me.'

'How on earth could he have done that?' gasped Penny.

'He was always threatening it—on the grounds of my lax moral behaviour, even at that age—but I knew him well enough to know what I could get away with. He actually saw himself as a connoisseur, his vanity in that area was such that I would have been out on my ear even to question his taste. I could have done as I pleased later, when Lexy was older, but I'd already made a pact with myself to touch nothing until he was out of our lives for good.'

'Dominic, I'm so sorry. I——'

'Penny, why do you always feel obliged to apologise whenever you get me talking about the past?' he exclaimed impatiently. 'After all, you're the one asking the questions.'

'I know, but. . .well, it all seems so sad.'

'Does it?' he enquired coldly, glancing around him

and signalling a waiter for the bill. 'It would have seemed a lot sadder had Lexy and I been left penniless orphans. . . Shall we go?' he added as the waiter arrived.

Penny found herself mulling over his words as he paid the bill, stunned by their dismissive bitterness.

'You can't say money made your childhood any happier,' she stated, as he opened the car door for her outside the restaurant.

'No, but it gave us a comfortable cushion on which to be miserable,' he answered, getting in and starting up the car. 'I'd have thought that fairly self-evident, even to someone cushioned so substantially by money that she doesn't have to work at anything more than the occasional charity.'

And that was just the first lie from which she was reaping her rewards, thought Penny, stunned. She hurriedly cast all thought from her mind of any potential result from the second.

'The next time we're down in Palma I must show you the cathedral. It was begun in the thirteenth century but not completed until well into the sixteenth. . .though perhaps you're not interested in that sort of thing.'

'Why—because you've decided to cast me in the role of the spoiled, rich ignoramus, incapable of appreciating life's finer things?' she lashed out, uncertain against which of them she was directing the bulk of her anger.

'If I've misjudged you, perhaps you'd be interested in seeing my etchings tonight?' he drawled.

'Yes—I'd be most interested,' she hissed rashly.

He gave a soft, infuriating chuckle. 'Are you sure that's wise—you being a woman contemplating the proposal of another, I mean?'

'I was under the impression I was being offered a cultural experience,' she retaliated, even more rashly.

'I suppose I could throw in a bit of that too, if you insist—but no, culture wasn't at all what I had in mind.'

Hating to admit defeat, but realising her rash outbursts would only result in her being left open to yet more of the same, Penny maintained an uncompromising silence for the rest of the journey.

It wasn't until they had negotiated the worst of the hairpin bends of the steeply rising then sharply falling road that led eventually to the Formentor Peninsula, that the first drops of rain began falling.

'Juana was right,' muttered Dominic, at last breaking the frigid silence. He pressed a button on the dashboard which brought the convertible roof of the car sliding silently into place around them.

By the time they reached the villa, the rain was dropping in an unbroken sheet from sombre skies.

'I can't say I remember having seen rain like this here before,' he said, switching off the engine. He turned to her. 'Penny, you wouldn't mind nipping into the house to see if you could find me an umbrella, would you? I hate getting my hair wet.'

It was his completely deadpan tone that held her frozen in an instant of shock—then she disolved into laughter.

'Come on,' she challenged through her chuckles. 'I'll race you in!'

She was drenched in the few seconds it took for her to reach the front door. When she turned to look for him, she found him sauntering towards her, his head thrown back as the rain gushed down on him.

'You're mad!'

'I told you I like rain,' he called back. 'Care to dance?'

She leaned weakly against one of the marble columns, watching as he executed a clowning dance before joining her.

'Your hair's wet,' she laughed up at him as they entered the house.

'Oh, my God—no!' Dominic groaned, clutching theatrically at his head.

'You *are* mad,' she sighed exasperatedly. 'Completely and utterly.' Then she was shrieking in protest as he caught hold of her, shaking his head and spraying drops of rain all over her.

'No—don't!' he exclaimed, as she made to break free. 'There's something I need to check up on.'

Before Penny had time to realise what was happening, let alone register any protest, his arms were holding her fully and his mouth was covering hers. Yet when his arms repositioned her more firmly against him, and when his lips began moving in probing sureness on hers, she realised exactly what was happening, and she registered not the slightest protest.

Her arms slipped around him, her hands spreading against the muscled firmness of his back, and as her lips parted beneath his they tasted the heady sweetness of passion and instantly craved for more.

'You're wet,' he groaned softly against her mouth, his own silencing any reply as it continued its fevered exploration.

And when his fingers deftly undid her button-through top, the only moves she made were to accommodate him and then to stretch her arms up and around his neck. Each new sensation bombarding her she welcomed with a total lack of any inhibition, a small, sharp cry of pleasure escaping her even when his hands moved to cup her breasts.

But when his fingers began their delicate search against her flesh, the excitement they awoke in her turned pleasure to a need and then to a powerful demand that stirred a spark of alertness in her even as its drug threatened to overwhelm her.

'Dominic, I. . . Please,' she gasped, her incoherent words reflecting the chaos within her.

'You're not drunk now, Penny,' he whispered hoarsely. 'You never were, but I had to check.'

'To check what?' she groaned, the glimmer of sanity striving to gain hold in her losing ground to the allure of an instinctive knowledge that here in his arms she would find the answer to the need aching through her.

'That the effect of our first accidental kiss hadn't been a figment of my imagination,' he whispered distractedly against lips loath to be parted from his. He withdrew his head slightly from hers, the darkness of passion burning in his eyes as he gazed down at her. 'I hate to stop, my sweet, but I think we ought to take ourselves off somewhere more suitable. . . Tempted though I am, the hall floor isn't an ideal place for making love.'

It was the unmistakable fact he was stating in those huskily whispered words that restored her sanity in one blinding flash, but it was the paralysing shock of her own behaviour that made speech impossible for her—that led her to walk through the marbled halls beside him like an automaton, her unfeeling hand locked in his.

When he stopped she felt him turn her towards him, and the touch of his fingers on her cheek.

'You're crying,' he stated, the words almost expressionless. 'I should have given into temptation and made love to you right there and then.'

'I'm sorry,' she whispered through frozen lips, scarcely hearing her own reflex words through the pall of dazed disbelief still paralysing her thought processes.

'Are you sure I'm the person you should be apologising to? This time you've only been unfaithful to him in your thoughts, but the next time it will be by your deeds.'

CHAPTER FOUR

THREE days, thought Penny, weary reluctance dragging her footsteps towards the kitchen. Three days of gale-force winds and torrential rain that even her limited knowledge told her must be unusual—if not unique—for this sunshine island. Three days with neither sign nor word of Lexy, and not even the presence of Juana or the maid as relief from a companion who regarded verbal combat as a form of relaxation and who could, when the mood took him, innocently discuss the weather while his eyes lazily stripped the clothing from her body.

'I thought it was your turn to cook breakfast this morning,' was the accusation with which Dominic greeted her appearance.

'You should have thought of that before being so rude about the lunch I produced,' she retorted, and was instantly furious with herself for rising without hesitation to his proffered bait—perhaps, just perhaps, she would one day learn to think before opening her mouth!

'It wasn't my intention to be rude. I merely pointed out that it was inedible,' he replied, juggling toast from the toaster to the warming drawer and refilling the toaster with a casual efficiency she found immensely galling. 'A lightly grilled slab of stewing beef isn't exactly my idea of the perfect lunch.'

'I've already told you I mistook it for steak!' she exclaimed. Scant minutes in his presence and already she was well on the way to losing her temper!

'My, you do seem to have got out of bed on the

wrong side this morning, Penny,' he murmured, removing eggs from the pan on the cooker before him. 'Don't tell me this freak weather's still disturbing your sleep?'

For once managing to guard her tongue, and then only by gritting her teeth quite painfully, Penny busied herself stacking crockery and cutlery on to the trolley. The truth was she hadn't had a decent night's sleep since the bad weather had started, she accepted wearily. Not that the weather had anything to do with it, apart from offering her the odd brief moment of distraction on the first night from the furious churning of the thoughts that had kept her remorselessly from sleep throughout it.

She watched in silence as he began loading up the trolley, willing objectivity into the eyes that travelled from the taut, muscled broadness of his shoulders to the luxuriant darkness of his hair and then on to the chiselled uniformity of his handsome features. The ghastly thing was that she had spent the best part of a year worried sick about the possibility—no, the probability—that she was frigid, and now she was reduced to losing sleep over the fact that she most certainly wasn't. She watched as he transferred the boiled eggs into a napkin-lined basket, noticing the strong whiteness of the teeth biting gently in concentration against the fullness of his bottom lip as he did so. And well might she be losing sleep, she thought dejectedly as her treacherous stomach gave a rolling lurch—he was argumentative, openly delighted in infuriating her, and was self-possessed way beyond the point of arrogance. . .and she fancied him like mad!

'A peseta for them,' he murmured, his eyes rising without warning to hers.

'If you must know, I was wondering how much longer you could possibly drag that out—I'm starving.'

Though her tone achieved the required haughtiness, her cheeks unfortunately flamed like beacons.

'Glad to hear it,' he replied, his mocking eyes moving slowly from one glowing cheek to the other. 'You trundle this lot into the dining-room while I grab the coffee-pot.'

Given the choice, she fumed defeatedly, she would settle for frigidity any day over this decidedly alarming physical attraction towards a man she hardly knew and didn't even like most of the time.

It was against the absent Lexy that she began levelling all her pent-up frustrations as they took breakfast. Where the hell was she? Probably doubled up with laughter somewhere at the thought of what she was suffering here, imagined Penny sourly, her friend having no doubt known all along the likely outcome.

'Don't you think you ought to try contacting Lexy?' she demanded, impatience spilling into her words. 'After all, she should have been here two days ago.'

'I tried ringing her on and off last night, right up until two this morning, in fact,' he replied, his tone sharp. 'I also tried several other places she might have been—again without success.' He was frowning deeply as he picked up his cup and drank from it. 'And I plan contacting a few other people just as soon as we've finished breakfast.'

Something in his tone brought Penny's eyes to his face, and the worry she saw etched in every line of it startled her.

'There's no need to panic,' she chided, touched despite herself. 'Something tells me that this new——' She broke off in the nick of time, appalled at how casually she had almost let slip the very thing Lexy wanted kept from him.

'Well?' Dominic demanded, his eyes sharp with suspicion. 'What, precisely, tells you what?'

'That. . .well, she's obviously heard about the bad weather here,' Penny gabbled as the tell-tale colour rose steadily in her cheeks, 'and she's sensibly decided to postpone coming until it clears.'

Those shrewd eyes of his once again swept from one colourful cheek to the other before he spoke.

'And you—a friend of hers—don't find it odd that it didn't occur to her to pick up the phone and inform us of this sensible decision of hers?' he enquired, the words dripping ice.

Penny's heart sank. Punctuality and impeccable good manners were Lexy's hallmarks, and it would take something quite extraordinary to suspend either in her. This Peter Langton really must be someone even more special than she had suspected, she realised with a small *frisson* of anxiety.

'You never know—perhaps this bad weather's affecting the telephones,' she muttered, unconvincingly even to her own ears.

'There's absolutely nothing wrong with the telephones here,' he snapped, his eyes flashing danger signals as he added, 'And if she's up to something which you know about, I suggest you tell me here and now, before I waste hours attempting to track her down.'

'Why on earth should she be up to something?' blustered Penny. 'Anyone would think she was a child, the way you talk, instead of a grown woman.'

'And even as a child Lexy was never irresponsible,' Dominic informed her acidly. 'Before I knew I'd manage to get here, I arranged for her to choose furnishing samples and bring them over to discuss with the hotel manager. Lexy knows Miguel's arranged to spend some time in Spain as from the end of this week.'

'But she also knows you're here now,' protested Penny, again with a disturbing lack of conviction according to her own ears.

'For God's sake!' he exploded. 'She knows me well
enough to know that despite having the ultimate say
I'd never dream of imposing anything on my manager
without consulting him first!' He slammed his fist down
on the table with a force that rattled the crockery and
almost had Penny jumping out of her skin. 'You know
where she is, don't you?' he accused harshly.

'No!' she exclaimed, relieved at last to be actually
speaking the truth. 'Dominic, honestly, I've no idea
where she might be.'

But he hadn't believed her; of that she had little doubt.

She had spent the rest of the morning browsing
listlessly in the book-lined study, torn by twin feelings
of guilt and loyalty—the guilt jolting to the forefront
each time the extension phone in the room emitted the
strangled half-ring indicating that Dominic was making
yet another call in his attempt to track down his sister.

'Damn it, Lexy—how could you do this to me?' she
groaned softly as the phone yet again gave out its
accusing little ping.

Incredible though it might seem, she must have
moved in with Peter Langton, reasoned Penny desperately. And it really was none of Dominic's business
what Lexy chose to do, she told herself firmly, returning the book she had been leafing through to its shelf.
Then she leaned her head wearily against the row of
books as the guilt she had been so assiduously suppressing suddenly broke free and washed over her.

The dreadful thing was that he was so unquestionably
and deeply worried. . .just as she herself would have
been had she not know the truth.

Now thoroughly racked by guilt, she made her way
to the kitchen, finding welcome distraction from the
cringe-making memories of her previous day's attempts
as she contemplated making lunch.

They were running very low on food, she told herself after a quick search, guilt nagging persistently within her. And it nagged on unabated while she made up a cheese salad with the bits and pieces she could find and then placed some stale bread in the oven in an attempt to revive it.

'Are you doing lunch?'

'Yes,' replied Penny, starting visibly at the unexpected sound of his voice. 'Is there any chance of our doing a bit of shopping?' she added, composing herself. 'We seem to be running out of food. . . Dominic, is something wrong?' she asked, thrown by the oddly strained look on his face as he approached her.

'Yes,' he rasped, halting so close to her that their bodies almost touched. 'Your apparent lack of interest in my sister's whereabouts.' He grasped her by the shoulders, his fingers biting into her flesh. 'You didn't even ask if I'd managed to contact her! You're either a lousy friend, or you know where she is. Which is it, Penny?'

'Dominic, you're hurting me!'

'Yes, and I shall go on doing so until I get a reply,' he informed her quietly.

'Just who the hell do you think you are?' she demanded, wincing with pain as her frantic struggles resulted in a bruising increase of pressure from his fingers. 'Dominic. . .let go of me, for heaven's sake!'

'Where is Lexy?'

'I've already *told* you,' she shrieked, terrified. 'I don't know where she is!'

'I don't believe you.'

'Dominic, you'll just *have* to believe me,' she croaked, his chillingly expressionless tones terrifying her even more than the violence of his hold on her. 'Brotherly concern is one thing, but for heaven's sake,

Dominic, Lexy's *twenty-three*!' Her words ended on a shriek of pure fear as he shook her with savage force.

'I'm beginning to wonder whether you know her at all,' he raged, his eyes black with fury. 'Anyone who knows her knows that if Lexy says "I'll probably see you around six", they discount the "probably" and the "around". . .that she'll be there on the dot of six because that's the way she is, always has been and always will be!'

'Yes, I know that, but. . .' But what? Penny couldn't argue with a single word he had hurled at her.

'But what?' he demanded, the unrelenting pressure of his fingers making her feel slightly queasy from pain.

'Dominic, you're hurting me. . . I can't think straight,' she pleaded hoarsely.

He eased his hold a barely perceptible fraction.

'Apart from her obsession about time-keeping, my sister also happens to be an exceptionally wealthy woman in her own right,' he rasped.

'What on earth has that got to do with anything?' exclaimed Penny, then gave a sudden groan of incredulity. 'Dominic, you can't be suggesting someone would *kidnap* her, or anything as crazy as that?'

'There's nothing in the least crazy about it. Anyone that way inclined would be justified in considering it worthwhile,' he replied tonelessly. 'There are also other, easier ways of relieving the wealthy of their money. . . Or have you forgotten what happened to your friend Erica?'

'Erica? But that was drugs,' croaked Penny, her blood running cold.

'Yes. And how those involved must have rued the day their goose took an accidental overdose and thus put paid to their endless supply of golden eggs,' he stated grimly, his grip on her suddenly easing.

'Dominic, please. . .you've got to stop thinking

along these dreadful lines,' Penny pleaded, guilt swamping her. 'I had no idea you'd start thinking like this——'

'Otherwise you wouldn't have lied to me?' he enquired, a chill softness to his words.

'I didn't lie, I. . .' She took a deep breath, knowing she had to do something to stop him torturing himself as he was. 'I'm pretty sure there's a new man in Lexy's life.' She gave a shiver of fear as she felt his body tense. 'Someone pretty special, judging by how secretive she's being about him.'

'Why didn't you mention this before?' he demanded icily.

'Because. . . I've just told you,' she protested disjointedly. 'She doesn't want anyone to know about——'

'What's this man's name?'

'I don't know.'

'You're lying, Penny,' he whispered with soft menace. 'Did she specifically ask you not to mention him to me?'

'No. . . I. . .she just didn't seem to want *anyone* to know,' she stammered.

'So you thought it best not to tell me, either?'

She nodded, that soft menace still in his voice making words impossible.

'And you think my sister might be in love?'

Again she nodded.

'Well, just let's hope, for your sake, that's the way it is,' he said, suddenly jerking her against the length of him. 'And now—what about us, Penny?' he mocked. 'Are you still kidding yourself you're going to remain technically faithful to poor what's-his-name, or are you prepared to have a stab at making all my dreams come true?'

Penny's head was still reeling from trying to cope

with both his sudden action and his utterly confusing switch to another subject entirely.

'If that's your idea of a joke, I don't find it particularly funny,' she eventually managed, though only just, thanks to the painful thuddings of her heart—a relentless tom-tom of a beat he couldn't possibly be unaware of given the suffocating closeness of their bodies.

'Of course you don't,' he whispered, his hands sliding slowly down her body to the hollow of her back. 'But you find it exciting, though, don't you, Penny?' he coaxed huskily as his hands slid further, his fingers splaying against the firm curve of her buttocks.

Mesmerised, she could only shake her head in futile denial of the powerful blasts of excitement surging through her.

'You're lying again, Penny,' Dominic chided, his soft chuckle turning to a sharp groan of desire as the sensuous play of his hands drew her body against the sudden potent arousal of his.

'Please, Dominic,' she whispered distractedly, her every sense responding with intoxicated abandon to the unequivocal message of his body.

'With pleasure,' he breathed, his mouth for an instant gentle on hers before parting it with a bruising savagery that denied all knowledge of gentleness.

For one stunned instant she was passive in his arms, then she was fighting him with all the strength she possessed—her fists trying to pummel on the chest against which they were trapped, her body twisting frantically for escape from the manacing strength of his. Yet even as she fought she was responding to the allure of him, her every sense being assailed by an impossible mixture of razor-sharp excitement and softly melting langour.

'No!' she cried out in panic as those plundering lips relinquished hers to burn their hot-breathed trail of devastation against her throat. 'Dominic, please!' she begged, her hands rising to tug frantically in his hair as the sharpness of his teeth grazed against her flesh.

It was as his hands reached up to cover hers and force them from his head that his mouth suddenly became gentle, anointing where his passion had punished with the soft moistness of its caress.

'Do I frighten you, Penny?' he asked hoarsely, his eyes dark enigmatic pools as he raised his head.

Yet the small *frisson* of fear both his words and the expression in his eyes initiated in her became transformed to tremulous shivers of excitement as his mouth once again took possession of hers. And the arms he had placed round his neck tightened in welcome even as she sensed the bruising savagery of his first kiss straining to break through the delicate veneer of tenderness he now applied to this second. And though the swollen rawness of the lips against which his now beguiled should have been further cause for caution, it was the trembling, aching sweetness with which that kiss filled her that left her completely without defence.

Her hands began their own caressing when his impatiently freed her blouse to slip beneath it and caress against her skin. And this time, when his mouth unleashed the full ferocity of his need on hers, she met him unflinchingly, her arms tightening around his neck as though to trap him forever to her.

'This gets better every time,' he groaned dazedly against her lips. 'But you know where it has to lead?'

Her answer was in the unhibited seeking of her mouth against his.

'You do know, don't you, Penny?' he persisted, drawing his head from hers.

There was a cold, glittering darkness in the eyes now peering down into hers, yet it was to the blatant heat of desire in the taut body enslaving hers that she responded.

'Yes. . . I know,' she whispered, impatiently drawing his head back to hers.

It was in that moment their breaths mingled before their lips finally met that she felt his resistance.

'But not now, my sweet seductress. . .not right now.'

'But why not?' she exclaimed, the words of protest winging from her of their own volition even as she became aware of the sudden tension stilling him.

His body returned to life as he inhaled slowly and deeply, then the sensation of his chest expanding against her—as though part of her own body—was gone as his hands reached up and caught hers by the wrists, then drew her arms from around him in a gesture of total rejection.

'Because, for one thing, lunch awaits,' he replied, the calculated coldness in the voice that had seconds before whispered with the fire of passion freezing her to stunned incomprehension. 'And, for another, you've yet to tell me the name of this new man in my sister's life.'

It was the sharp pain of his momentarily tightening grasp on her wrists before releasing them that brought the first tentative stir to her frozen senses. She took a step back from him, her eyes huge with bemusement as part of her still refused to accept what was happening. Then, when bemusement became horror, her mind stalled its acceptance of reality by resorting to dreams of the miracle that could turn back the clock and erase what it balked at facing.

Then there was nothing but the slow burn of humiliation seeping its sluggish way throughout her.

'Only the coldest and most calculating of monsters could do what you've just done,' she croaked, her mouth like sandpaper.

'Really?' he drawled, his eyes narrowed and watchful.

'Really! To pretend passion. . .just to get a name out of me. . .'

'If it weren't so ludicrously naïve, your assessment of my acting skills would be rather flattering,' he murmured in that same coldly drawling voice. 'But unfortunately the physical manifestations of desire aren't something a man can summon up to order. Or, to put it crudely——'

'Oh, I'm sure you can put it very crudely,' lashed out Penny, the anger now smouldering within her the only thing holding her together as a devastating trembling began racking her body. 'But you needn't bother.'

His acquiescent shrug was in direct contrast to the harsh, humourless laugh it accompanied. 'Judging by your accusation, I feel I should bother. . . But rather than offend your sensibilities, I'll put it another way.'

There was no way she could have anticipated his next move, and by the time her outraged mind had digested what he had done his hands had returned to his sides, having already reached out and cupped her breasts, each thumb having lightly caressed against the rigid peaks outlined sharply beneath the soft material of her blouse.

'You see, it works both ways,' he murmured, as though explaining the workings of a toy to a child. 'Granted, the female body doesn't signal its desire quite as flamboyantly as that of the male. . .but it sure as hell does it, wouldn't you agree?'

For several seconds Penny fought to keep her mouth shut, for once aware that had she opened it nothing more than a rage of gibberish would have come from it. She was completely trapped—in unfamiliar surroundings in a completely strange country, in a lie enforced on her by friendship and in her ludicrous, totally inexplicable physical entrapment by a man whom she positively loathed!

And then, as though by a miracle, her head suddenly cleared, replacing anger and humiliation with giddy elation. . . She could always leave!

Her shoulders squared perceptibly as she faced him, and she almost managed a smile.

'There's cheese salad for lunch, which your sensitive tastebuds will no doubt reject in disgust. And there's bread warming in the oven—though I dare say that's done to a cinder by now.' She turned on her heel and marched through the door.

She was tempted to dance a small jig on her way to her room, but was still too giddy from relief to risk it.

Yes, she was taking the coward's way out, but she didn't care. She had come close—within a whisker, to be perfectly honest—of making the most colossal fool of herself, and now she was making her escape. Perhaps Lexy was right after all about Leos throwing a mental wobbly over being made to look foolish, she conceded indulgently as she entered her room—this one certainly didn't take at all kindly to it.

She got down a case and opened it up, then froze, her smile faltering to a tense grimace. Lexy! If Lexy wasn't around she would have nowhere to stay, and furthermore the rest of her clothes were at Lexy's place and it would probably be freezing in London by now!

'What exactly do you think you're doing?'

She swung round to find Dominic lounging in the doorway, an expression of irritation on his handsome features.

'I'm leaving.'

'Really? And where were you planning on going?'

'Back to London, of course,' she snapped, opening a drawer and removing clothes from it. Lexy was bound to have turned up by the time she got back, she told herself, choosing to ignore the niggling inner voice immediately querying such unfounded confidence.

'I see. . . You plan swimming down to Palma, do you?'

Penny swung round, flinging the clothes in her hands down on the bed.

'What's that supposed to mean?' she demanded, furious with herself for responding with a sharp stab of alarm to his taunting words.

'Well, you can't possibly drive,' he murmured, his tone oozing reasonableness. 'There are rockfalls and God only knows what else blocking the road between here and Pollensa, and then there are several areas of severe flooding further south. . . Didn't you know?'

'Of course I didn't know!' she wailed, flopping down on to the bed in despair. 'The weather's been atrocious, but. . .' She broke off with a hopeless shrug.

'Come along and have some lunch——'

'I don't want any lunch!' she hissed, on the verge of tears with frustration and disappointment. Was nothing in her life ever going to go smoothly again?

There was disdain in the cold eyes that flickered over her dejected figure.

'If it's any consolation, I wouldn't have allowed you to leave even had the weather been good.'

'You wouldn't. . .you——' She floundered, unable to believe her ears. 'My God, just who do you think you are?'

'A man who has a sister he loves and about whom he happens to be extremely worried,' he replied, and it was the hint of an underlying tone of utter desperation in those otherwise chillingly expressionless words that nudged aside Penny's anger and frustration to leave her with nothing but the wretchedness of an indescribable guilt.

'Dominic, I know you love her,' she whispered, that

guilt chastening her words. 'And knowing her fixation about turning up when she says she will, I'd have been worried too had I not been aware that there was something out of the ordinary happening in her life right now. She said practically nothing, yet the way she did speak told me at once that this man was different—no, hear me out. . . Please,' she pleaded as he gave an angry exclamation. 'The few men Lexy doesn't cold-shoulder as being after her money she treats in a most cavalier fashion. She tells her friends *everything* about them. . .things the men concerned would probably want to curl up and die if they ever got to know——'

'I'm not in the least interested in how my sister chooses to discuss men with her friends,' Dominic cut in dismissively, his eyes flashing anger.

'For heaven's sake, can't you understand what I'm saying?' exclaimed Penny. 'I honestly suspect this man has achieved the impossible—that he's swept Lexy off her feet! And all I can say is good luck to them!'

'And she's suddenly so secretive that she won't even tell you his name?' he drawled contemptuously.

'Yes,' muttered Penny, her eyes avoiding his.

'I've never heard such a load of romantic drivel in my entire life,' he spat, striding towards her. 'I know my sister well enough to know that, whatever her feelings for him, no man could sweep her off her feet, as you put it, to the extent of rendering her incapable of picking up a phone and explaining her absence.' He reached out, taking her by the shoulders and hauling her swiftly to her feet. 'I'm giving you till the morning, Penny,' he snarled, his eyes black with rage. 'And if my London contacts haven't come up with what I need, I'm getting it out of you!'

'How—with the thumbscrews you carry around in case of just such an emergency?' she yelled, struggling like one possessed.

'Why should I inflict pain on you when I can get what I want out of you by other means?' he said softly, sinking the fingers of one hand into her hair and jerking back her head. 'And with such ease?' he taunted, crushing her body to his as he kissed her with a slow sensuality that suspended her ability to reason for just long enough for that mind-sapping kiss to have ended by the time the idea of putting up a struggle was beginning to occur to her.

There was a mocking half-smile on his mouth as he drew away from her which deepened as his eyes moved slowly from hers to the erect outline of her nipples against the soft material of her blouse and then back to hers.

'And now for lunch,' he murmured, releasing her, then turning and leaving the room.

Penny's eyes sank to where his had so briefly lingered, a deep wash of scarlet painting her cheeks. Her body had become an enemy over which she had no control. And as for her loyalty to Lexy, which had landed her in this morass of humiliation, surely there had to be some limit as to how far she was expected to carry it?

CHAPTER FIVE

THE rest of that day and the night that followed were hours spent in heart, soul and mind searching. And her searching led her back to her earliest years and to the inevitability of the solitude that came with being an only child in a family constantly on the move because of her father's career. It had been the instinctive recognition of their kindred inner solitude that had drawn together herself, Lexy, Sarah and Erica, bonding four widely differing personalities into an oddly undemanding, yet unquestioningly supportive friendship that doggedly survived despite years of neglect and separation. Now there was only Lexy and Sarah left with the ability to pierce her solitude within the unspoken bounds of their friendship.

And now Dominic was barging uninvited through her shell, disregarding all those unspoken rules constructed to preserve it intact, and ultimately forcing her to rethink values which had been formed over a lifetime.

Throughout those hours she found her thoughts veering off at the wildest of tangents till at one point she could take it no more and had found herself, at two in the morning, packed and dressed and ready to risk trying to drive to Palma, before reason had belatedly returned to her.

With limbs leaden with weariness and eyes hollowed and dark-ringed, she had risen from her bed shortly after dawn had staggered drunkenly across sullen skies. Cold and dejected and with a disruptively new set of values struggling to form within her, she lay soaking in

70

a hot bath and agonised over her now-incredible past smugness.

How easily she had looked down on as weak those women who had become trapped in the snare of the same violent physical attraction in which she now found herself. And even when the man now ensnaring her had been discussed those years ago, how easily she had pooh-poohed the very idea of any man possessing an animal magnetism that could have such an effect. And what about Rupert and Linda? Had it been a manifestation of that same overwhelming force she was now experiencing that had negated Rupert's claims of love and Linda's of friendship?

It was only when she was dressed and sitting huddled on her bed, wrestling with the problem of whether her loyalty to Lexy should take precedence over her compassion for Dominic's obvious anxiety, that it occurred to her that her feelings towards Rupert had become reduced to no more than what constituted a vague twinge of compassion.

Hell, she hadn't even been in love with Rupert! she told herself exasperatedly, leaping down from the bed. She could have saved herself this whole damned trip, she remonstrated illogically with herself as she dawdled listlessly towards the kitchen in search of the strongest coffee she could possibly brew.

The sight greeting her as she walked through the open door was that of Dominic slumped on a chair at the scrubbed table, his head cushioned against the arms sprawled out across its surface, and sound asleep.

On bare feet now unpleasantly aware of the coldness of the marble beneath them, she crept towards him. The pressure of the arm against which his cheek lay had softened the sharply defined fullness of his mouth almost to a pout.

Lexy's big, bad, beautiful brother, she chanted

silently to herself while the molten heat of a burgeoning longing rippled through her veins. Big and beautiful he most certainly was, she accepted, just as she accepted with an almost fatalistic resignation the feelings now bombarding her. . .the most physically beautiful man she had ever seen. But bad too, she forced herself to accept as the heavy dark sweep of his lashes seemed to grow irresistibly lusher and richer beneath her mesmerised gaze. And not merely the badness to be chuckled over by an adoring sister, but a calculating ruthlessness that made the animal magnetism of which he was so utterly aware a dangerous weapon he would use, without so much as a thought, as a means to his ends.

She gave an involuntary shiver as she remembered the latent violence beneath the cool deliberation with which he had demonstrated his power over her and delivered his threat. Yet even as she was remembering she was consciously resisting the temptation to reach out and smooth back the dark hair tumbling across his forehead.

She turned away with a small exclamation of self-disgust, then tried to calm herself with the reminder that she was half dead on her feet and in desperate need of the boost of caffeine strong coffee would supply.

She reached across his prone form for the coffee-jug beside him, her gaze skimming from the stubbled darkness of his chin towards his eyes at the precise moment they suddenly opened, wide and watchful.

'I was just about to make some coffee,' she said, pleased, though more than a little started, to hear how completely ordinary her tone had sounded.

'Good. . . I could do with one,' he muttered, his words still slurred with sleep.

'The rain seems to have eased a little,' she said, the

stark strain now in her tone reflected in the jerkiness of her movements as she filled and switched on the kettle and then rinsed the jug.

'Yes. . .but the weather doesn't alter the fact that you're trapped here, does it, Penny?' he observed expressionlessly, tilting back in his chair to watch her every move over his shoulder.

Determined not to respond to his blatant goading, she prepared the coffee in silence.

'Does it, Penny?' he repeated as she brought fresh cups to the table.

As she turned to get the coffee his hand reached out, his fingers encircling her wrist in a pressureless band.

'If you're trying to frighten me, you're wasting your time,' she told him quietly, making no attempt to free herself.

'Am I?' he murmured, the softness of his words contrasting sharply with the strength with which he suddenly pulled her down on to his knee. 'I'm not very often wrong about people, Penny,' he continued, the silkiness of menace now in his tone. 'But let's hope I am about you, because if I'm not I'd be very frightened if I were in your shoes.'

'I fail to see any logic in your threats,' Penny stated, the unnatural calmness in her words masking the thudding of a heart that was like a caged violence against her chest. 'You've stooped low enough to threaten me sexually, yet the unfortunate fact of my physical response to you—and which you've taken such gentlemanly delight in pointing out to me—tends to make any such threat a little empty, wouldn't you say?'

'Bravo, Penny, bravo!' Dominic drawled softly, his incipient beard sharp against her skin as he nuzzled the nape of her neck before rising abruptly to his feet and depositing her back on hers. 'But you're a little behind the times.'

'Oh—in what way?' she snapped, busying herself by pouring the coffee in an attempt to regain a measure of equilibrium and to mask how thoroughly unsettled she was.

'Thank you,' he muttered, accepting a cup, his eyes coldly watchful as he towered over her. 'I'm expecting a call from a friend in London. He's checking on something he heard, but there was something in his tone that got my sixth sense working over-time. . .something over and above the fact that he was uncharacteristically loath to discuss what it was he had heard, and felt obliged to check before passing it on to me.'

Penny took her coffee to the table and sat down, curving her hands around the cup for warmth. She had a pretty good idea what the rumour was this friend had heard, and understood only too well his reluctance to tell Dominic exactly with whom it was Lexy was involved.

'In fact, he was every bit as loath to discuss the subject with me, Penelope dear, as you are. . . Odd, isn't it?' he murmured with venomous sweetness.

'Well, I dare say your friend will ring back with whatever it is you want,' she said with forced bright-ness, inwardly dreading the moment. 'Then all your worries will be over.'

'What a comfort you are to have around,' he mut-tered sarcastically, flinging his tall frame down on the chair beside hers.

Penny's eyes flickered towards his darkly shadowed face and immediately away as the skin at the back of her neck began tingling with the memory of the brief roughness of its touch.

'Mind you, if my worries were all over, I could settle down to finding out whether or not you're the one I'll finally succumb to,' he drawled softly. 'Mind you, that would only create another set of worries to plague me, were I to—wouldn't you say, Penny?'

Penny flashed him the most withering look that her feelings of total exhaustion allowed her to summon up. And despite her exhaustion, she was alert enough to detect a strange element of half-heartedness in his present baiting of her—as though his mind were on other matters.

'I wouldn't worry too much, if I were you,' she replied. 'Habits of a lifetime aren't that easily broken.'

'God, what a relief!' he exclaimed dourly. 'I'd always heard that love was one of those unpleasant occurrences that slunk up and took unsuspecting folks unawares. . . Are you actually telling me I'll have some choice in the matter when the time comes?'

'Dominic, I'm really not in the mood for this,' she replied wearily; she had no intention of being the butt of his sarcasm while he sought distraction from his groundless worries.

'But you know how I enjoy a lively discussion,' he protested with patently false innocence. 'No wonder my star-struck little sister made no attempt to bring us together. She must have realised how badly suited we'd be. I thrive on argument, but according to Lexy all Scorpios do——'

'You're *not* a Scorpio—Lexy is. You're a Libran, for heaven's sake,' snapped Penny, weariness sapping her of any sense of caution. 'And the reason she keeps any woman she cares about as far from your clutches as possible is because she's fully aware of your appalling record with women—as are the couple of friends unfortunate enough to have slipped through her protective net and fallen foul of your charms!'

'A Libran,' he murmured, as though hearing the word for the first time—an impossibility with Lexy as a sister. 'An appalling abuser of women. . . Well, well. I really must pay more attention to Lexy's astrological incantations in future. Tell me, Penny, are you by any chance a Libran too—an appalling abuser of men?'

'No, I'm not—I'm a Leo!' she blurted out in exasperation.

'Are you, now?' he chuckled. 'And what do they do—rip men to shreds with their pussy-cat claws?'

'I've really no idea,' she muttered, wondering if a subject existed that he couldn't eventually fan into a blazing row. 'I know practically nothing about astrology.'

'Neither do I—so what are we arguing about?'

'For heaven's sake, you're the one who's just said how he loves arguing!' she shrieked.

'So I did, and it's sweet of you to be so obliging,' he said softly, the quick glance he gave his watch only strengthening her feeling that his mind was on other things. 'So now let's discuss falling in love—it's such an uncharted area for me.'

'And one, therefore, that there's little point in your trying to discuss,' retorted Penny.

'But it's such fun learning from an expert,' he persisted, before his entire body suddenly froze rigid at the distant sound of a ringing phone. 'And now all my worries will be over, is that right, Penny?' he asked flippantly, but the darkness of the stubble on his chin accentuated the sudden pallor of his face before he turned from her and strode from the room.

'Dominic. . .what is it?' demanded Penny, fear prickling against her skin as he appeared in the kitchen doorway, a granite harshness immobilising the unmistakable rage suffusing his still-unshaven face.

'Don't ask me!' he rasped. 'Just——'

'What on earth are you saying?' she gasped, a sudden

surge of fear driving the breath from her lungs. 'Lexy. . .what's happened to her?'

'I wouldn't have thought even a bitch as stupid as you could be foolish enough to ask that,' he enunciated with barely controlled fury. 'Pack—we're leaving.'

Fear now a choking panic, she raced after him as he strode off.

'Dominic, please. . . I *beg* you! Tell me what's happened!'

He spun round as she reached his side, his face pale with unleashed rage.

'And I near as damn it begged *you*, didn't I, Penny?' he snarled, pushing her violently from his path as he strode on.

'Dominic, can't you understand there was nothing more I could possibly tell you?' she pleaded frantically, running to keep pace with him.

He stopped in his tracks, his clenched fist smashing against the wall scant inches from her with a sickening crunch.

'Get away from me,' he intoned hoarsely. 'That could so easily have been you.'

'If it makes you feel any better, then go on and hit me!' she cried wildly. 'But for God's sake tell me what's going on!'

'I'll tell you!' he raged, his control seeming to snap as he rounded on her, his fingers bruising against the flesh of her upper arms as he grasped her and lifted her almost off her feet. 'No. . .not here,' he hissed, evil in the eyes burning down into her. 'The light's not good enough. . . I want to be able to read every shade of every expression on your face.'

With his totally incomprehensible words only increasing her feelings of dread, Penny gave no resistance as he half dragged, half carried her to her room. Images of Lexy, laughing, rebellious, gentle, were flashing through her mind as the overhead lights came on. Then those images were blotted out by the ravaged gaze of the man gazing down at her upturned face and whose fingers now bit cruelly into her flesh.

'Now, let me read in your beautiful, lying face whether or not the name Peter Langton means anything to you,' he whispered, his eyes as cruel as his punishing fingers as they read the betrayal already staining her cheeks. 'Of course it does,' he snarled, flinging her from him with a voilence that knocked the breath from her as she landed sprawled across the bed. 'What can I possibly tell you about Lexy that you don't already know, you stupid, ignorant, criminally irresponsible bitch?'

As Penny struggled into a huddled sitting position, the realisation beginning to dawn on her chased away her feelings of panic and replaced them with ones of outrage. He had had her almost gibbering with fear over the possibility of something having happened to Lexy, but brotherly love, she now realised, had little to do with the violence of his rage —it was simply that his sister had had the temerity to get herself involved with a man whom this monstrously overbearing brother happened to dislike. In the light of what she had just witnessed, she could understand only too well why Lexy had broken habits of a lifetime and run for cover!

Her expression tight with disgust, she gazed up at his blackly scowling countenance.

'Why don't you take a look at yourself in that mirror over there?' she suggested through clenched teeth. 'I've seen three-year-olds display temper-tantrums similar to yours—but never an adult. Pick up a few things and smash them, then call me a few more names—that should help make you feel really great!'

She realised the instant the words were out how

stupid and, more to the point, how decidedly dangerous it was of her to have expressed her anger so
recklessly given his present mood; and the murderous
look in his eyes as he made a sudden start towards her
only strengthened that view. She felt the breath she
had been unconsciously holding burst from her as he
abruptly straightened, the hands clenching compulsively at his sides the only indication of the formidable
battle he was waging for control.

'You have fifteen minutes to get your things
together, then we're leaving,' he stated in a voice she
scarcely recognised; then he turned and left her.

For the second time in the space of hours, Penny
packed. And it was only when she had closed the
second of her cases that she gave a sudden groan of
anger and frustration. He had lied about the roads
being impassable! Had she just kept going in the small
hours of this morning she could have saved herself all
this!

'You lied to me about the roads, didn't you?' she
hurled at him in accusation as she dumped her bags by
the front door.

'How impertinent of me if I did—lying being your
exclusive prerogative,' he drawled, frowning as he
glanced down at her two pieces of luggage. 'Can't you
make do with one?'

Feeling inordinately inclined to fling herself on the
floor and have a trantrum of her own, Penny gritted
her teeth.

'No!'

He gave a shrug of annoyance, his eyes now scrutin-
ising her lightweight navy sweat-shirt and matching
skirt—the only relatively warm clothing she had
brought with her.

'Haven't you anything warmer than that?'

'No, I haven't!'

With an exclamation of impatience he strode off, appearing moments later with a heavy cream sweater of his own.

'You'd better put this on.'

Tempted to tell him what he could do with it, Penny nevertheless took it and put it on—she was frozen.

Furious that her body was choosing to respond to being in an article of his clothing much as it did to being in his arms, Penny picked up her bags and stormed through the door he had just opened. Yet once they were settled in his car she found herself puzzling over his unnecessary and obviously grudging concern for her well-being. . .it was hardly as though they would be tramping around in the open—and she would swelter on the plane dressed like this.

'Where are we going?' she demanded as it suddenly occurred to her that he was driving in completely the wrong direction.

'As I told you, the roads are blocked,' Dominic muttered, slipping down a gear as the car began sliding on the mud-washed road. 'Contrary to your belief, I wasn't lying—so we're having to go down by sea.'

'I wouldn't have thought they'd have any ferries running in weather like this,' said Penny, her heart thudding uncomfortably as her glance was drawn to the heaving grey of the sea.

'Wouldn't you?' he replied, his attention now entirely on the hazardous road conditions.

Penny said nothing—what was the point? Instead she made do with examining what could only be described as a crushing sense of disappointment now pervading her. Infuriating and argumentative though she had found him, it was pointless denying that she had liked him and that it had come as a sickening shock to her to discover the streak of vindictiveness in him that could make him behave so disgustingly—and all because his sister was involved with a man he happened to dislike. In fact, it went further than mere vindictiveness; it was her recognition of the barely dormant violence in him that had terrified her into complying with his orders to pack and leave. There was no earthly reason why she should be dragged along with him on a journey which no sane person would even contemplate in weather conditions such as these. . . She was here on his whim, as punishment for being an unwitting party to the cause of his unbalanced rage.

She glanced at his handsome, unyielding profile, the inevitable leap of excitement within her only magnifying the strength of her disappointment in him. She turned her face away. Why was it only now that she saw with such clarity how easily she could have loved him? Faults and all, as she had believed him to be until today, she could so easily have loved him. . .had been so close to loving him. And not just because of the powerful sexual feelings he awoke in her. . .though it seemed only right that feelings as overwhelming as those should go hand in hand with a readiness to love. And now that she knew him for the petty-minded and malevolent person he really was, there was no way he would ever be able to arouse such feelings in her again.

It was with a surge of relief, tinged with residual regret, that she turned to glance at him through new eyes and found their heads turning in unison.

So lost had she been in introspection that she had failed even to notice the slowing down of the car. It drew to a halt in almost the same instant their eyes met, his brooding and impenetrable, hers widening in sudden protest as the colour drifted slowly from her face.

'Don't worry, it probably isn't as bad as it looks,' he stated, his oddly detached words eventually penetrating the charged silence.

Penny tore her eyes from his, her fingers awkward as they fumbled against the seatbelt. No, it was probably a million times worse, she told herself with almost queasy apprehension—not that his words could possibly have had anything to do with what her stunned mind was so busily rejecting.

The wind was gusting strongly as they stepped out on to the quayside, but the rain was no more than an intermittent drizzle.

'Would you mind getting the things from the boot while I have a word with Don Jaime over there?' he asked, handing her the keys and striding off towards an elderly man waving to him from the bows of a magnificent white racing yacht—one of several boats still moored by the quay.

Having removed the luggage and relocked the boot, Penny gazed around, her eyes widening in disbelief at the sight of what must have been millions of pounds' worth of boats, seemingly abandoned to the mercy of the elements. Not that there weren't plenty of people around to tend these beautiful toys of the super-rich, she then realised wryly as she spotted several men in oilskins checking their battened-down and protected charges with meticulous care.

What in God's name was she doing here? she asked herself dejectedly; and what in God's name was she doing feeling that same ungovernable magnetism towards a man for whom she now felt no more than contempt?

Dragging her mind away from thoughts she had no stomach to examine, she looked down the length of the quay, frowning as she found the distraction she had so eagerly sought. The peninsula was known as a million-aires' playground, and all around were gleamingly elegant craft that proclaimed it to be every bit that. . .but nowhere was there anything that could by any stretch of the imagination be described as a common or garden ferry-boat!

Huddling herself into the welcome warmth of Dominic's sweater, she began walking towards the yacht on which Dominic had joined the man whom he had referred to as Don Jaime.

As she walked, the wind floated odd snatches of their conversation to her, and though she spoke no Spanish it became quite obvious to her that the conversation was a fairly heated one.

She hesitated uncertainly for a moment, then continued when both men began laughing, Dominic throwing back his head, his strong white teeth gleaming against his tan while the wind tossed his hair to a carefree wildness. All he needed was a dagger between his teeth and he would be the picture of the devil-may-care buccaneer incarnate, she mused bitterly.

They were deep in serious conversation by the time Penny reached the boat, and it was the aristocratic-looking Spaniard who spotted her first, his tone making it plain even to her that he was reprimanding Dominic for not acknowledging her presence.

'Sorry, I didn't see you down there,' Dominic called down to her, making shouted introductions as he leapt from the boat down on to the quayside beside her.

'If you have to put to sea with a madman, at least it's one who learned to handle a boat at the knee of a master,' the man called down to her in good English, his eyes twinkling. 'But no short cuts, eh, Dominic?'

'I'll stick to your route—that's a promise, Don Jaime,' chuckled Dominic, placing a sudden and heavily warning arm across Penny's shoulders as her face started giving signs that an exceptionally unpleasant understanding was beginning to dawn on her.

'Off you go now—just leave the keys in the car,'

called Don Jaime. 'And I'll make sure there's transport awaiting you at the other end.'

'Dominic——'

'We'd better get our things and get going,' he cut in, striding off and dragging her along with him. 'Where are the car keys?'

'In the car. Dominic——'

'We haven't time to talk,' he snapped, practically hauling her along to the car.

'Well, you'll just have to find some!' she exploded. 'Am I right in believing we're not travelling on a ferry-boat?'

'They don't run ferries from here,' he stated dismissively, releasing her. 'And besides, I've a perfectly adequate motor-launch of my own.'

'You've a. . . If you think I'm putting out to sea with you, you can think again!' she shrieked.

'I don't think it, I know it,' he retorted, swinging his leather duffle-bag over his shoulder and picking up one of her cases. 'Grab the other one, will you? We're in a hurry, and I need a hand free to keep tabs on you,' he added, that free hand grasping her by the arm.

'I'm not going,' she stated mutinously, obstinately standing her ground.

'Penny, I haven't time to argue with you——'

'You don't have to argue with me—I'm not going. You've already told me how stupid you think I am, but you underestimate me if you think I'm stupid enough to go to sea in a gale with a raving lunatic like you!'

'For God's sake, this is no more than a bit of strong wind!' he exclaimed. 'We've got a plane to catch, and you're coming with me. You can stall for as long as you like, but I'll throw you over my shoulder and carry you on to the boat if necessary. . .and the more time we waste the less time we'll have to keep to the route I've promised Don Jaime I'll stick to.'

Feeling trapped and nearer to breaking-point than she had ever been, Penny opened her mouth to scream abuse at him, then shut it defeatedly, her movements like those of a sleepwalker as she stooped and picked up her case.

The motor-launch to which Dominic had almost dismissively referred as 'perfectly adequate' turned out to be a gleaming blue and white vessel which, to Penny's increasingly glazed gaze, looked as though it would have been quite at home in a James Bond film. But by the time he had removed all the tailor-made protective tarpaulins and found oilskins for them both, Penny's gaze had taken on an even more fixed look. . .she was certain she was already feeling seasick.

She tried lying down in the huge, luxuriously appointed forward cabin, only to leap to her feet in terror as the motors hummed to life. The nearest she had ever been to boats was a dinghy in Brighton, and the sight of Dominic's tall, athletic and supremely confident figure at the helm brought her no shred of comfort. Despite the oilskins and the fact that he probably had the best technology money could buy at his fingertips, to her increasingly jaundiced eyes he now looked every inch the pirate plundering the high seas.

She turned away from the sight of him, the wind whipping sharply against her face, now desperately uncertain as to whether her queasiness was actually caused by incipient seasickness or the inescapable realisation that if she were going to die—which she was beginning to regard as almost a certainty—she would rather do so with his arms locked firmly around her.

CHAPTER SIX

'PENNY don't you think you should remove that sweater?' demanded Dominic, lowering the newspaper behind which he had been engrossed ever since take-off. 'You're going to feel the cold in London if you don't.'

Penny gave not the slightest acknowledgement of his words. She was never going to feel warm again, so the temperature in London was immaterial as far as she was concerned. And neither would her body ever recover from the violent buffeting of that life-threatening journey to Palma—never!

She turned her head to the window, peering out into the chill blue as she tried to close her mind to the fact that he had just tossed aside the paper and would no doubt start on her now that he had caught up with world events.

'I hate to intrude on this self-imposed vow of silence of yours,' he drawled in that familiar taunting tone of his, 'but there are one or two things we need to discuss—such as whether you've left your car at the airport.'

She wondered wearily how he would react to the knowledge that she didn't possess a car—simply because she had never been able to afford one. She was still wondering when suddenly her entire body tensed. What was far more the point, neither had she anywhere to live!

'Penny!' he growled warningly.

'No,' she muttered belatedly, her mind deciding it had had enough of all this trauma and obligingly placing itself on hold, allowing the exclamation of irritation which her reply had elicited from him to wash over her without so much as a ripple of response.

'All right—where, exactly, do you live in London, then?'

She almost responded to that with weak laughter, but the effort would have been too much, so she merely gave a non-committal shrug and pressed her forehead against the cool of the glass.

But her mind was dragged back with alacrity from its pleasant limbo the instant impatient fingers sank into her hair and forced her head round towards his.

'If you don't let go of me right now, I'll scream,' she informed him, her tone perfectly calm.

Their eyes locked—hers reflecting the unnatural calmness that had been in her words, his cool and inscrutable as his hand remained defiantly in position.

'Go ahead and scream,' he taunted softly, his eyes widening in momentary disbelief as her mouth opened to do so in that instant before his own covered and crushed it to silence.

'We could well end up spending the entire flight like this,' he eventually breathed against her lips. 'Or perhaps that's what you want.'

'I hate you!' she choked, despising herself for the eager excitement coursing through her.

His mouth returned to kissing hers, his lips coaxing yet impatient as his hands slid under her sweatshirt beneath his own bulky sweater to explore her trembling flesh.

'Try telling that to your body,' Dominic whispered barely coherently as his hands rose higher and cupped the tightly straining mounds of her breasts.

For several seconds Penny didn't even attempt to try, weakly giving herself up to the sweet intoxication of his marauding hands and the hot excitement his lips imparted to hers.

It was the intrusion of the soft voice over the intercom that jerked her suddenly back to reality, and that distracted him long enough for her to be able to pull free from him.

She looked at him in total panic as the erotic darkness in those heavy-lidded eyes seemed to will her back into his arms and every nerve in her body yearned to obey that call.

'I think I'm going to be sick!' she gasped, her starved lungs straining in protest as she came out with the only thing she could think of as a means of escape.

There was open alarm on his face as he quickly leapt up to make way as she barged past him and raced to safety.

Locked in the small cabin, she frantically splashed water against her now-burning cheeks as her lungs gasped great gulps of air and her sense churned in chaos.

She sank to her knees, burying her face in her dripping hands as she silently begged for freedom from the terrible nightmare in which she was trapped. All she wanted was to return to normality, she pleaded hopelessly. To what her life had been before Dominic Raphael had blasted his uninvited way into it. And hers had been a perfectly normal, run-of-the-mill life. It had had no more than its fair share of problems. . .right up until the day Ted Russell had called her into his office to tell her he had had an offer he couldn't afford to refuse for his small graphic design company in which she had worked so happily for the past three years. That part of the package entailed shedding all but his most senior staff was something she couldn't really blame Ted for, she thought miserably. But it had signalled the beginning of the most horrific change in the entire structure of her life. Close on its heels had come the truth about Rupert and Linda, and her having to leave the flat. . .

She hauled herself upright, bitterly asking herself who she thought she was fooling. The job, Rupert she could have coped with. . . It was taking up Lexy's offer—a stupid thing to do when she was homeless and jobless—that had ultimately sealed her fate.

'Penny, what the devil are you doing?'

She started, a sick, hopeless dread filling her at the angry roar of Dominic's voice and the impatient pummelling of his fist against the door. 'I'll get a steward to open this bloody door if——'

'For heaven's sake, I'll be out in a minute!' she yelled back; there had been a total lack of anything even approaching sympathy in his voice, she told herself angrily, then gave a soft groan of exasperation and despair that such a thought should even occur to her, let alone trouble her.

She dried her face and yanked open the door.

'Just leave me alone, will you?' she hissed as she was obliged to force her way past his bulk in the doorway before she could make for her seat.

'OK, whereabouts in London do you live?' he demanded as he joined her—as though the intervening minutes hadn't existed. 'And you can skip the "I'm going to scream" routine,' he added, turning to face her, 'because I don't fancy getting into a clinch with someone who's just spent the past few minutes throwing up——'

'I *haven't* been throwing up!' she objected indignantly before she could stop herself.

'I'm glad to hear it,' he drawled. 'But just let's say I can think of other ways you'd find less enjoyable of shutting you up, should you decide to——'

'I can think of none, short of breaking my neck,' she

blurted out—with infantile stupidity, she had to admit
the instant the words were out, given his calculatedly
insulting habit of pointing out to her just how much
she enjoyed his touch.

'Penny, for the last time—whereabouts do you live?'
he demanded, his patience plainly about to desert him.

'Nowhere.'

'Look, if this is your idea of a joke——'

'I'm *not* joking,' she protested, wondering how on
earth she was going to get herself out of this one
without yet again being utterly humiliated. 'I have
nowhere to live.'

For several seconds he glowered at her with open
disbelief, then his expression altered dramatically and
a groaned oath escaped him.

'Of course—you were living with loverboy,' he
drawled. 'The guy you love to the exclusion of all
others, or so the story goes. Damn it!'

Penny sank back against her seat, almost trembling
with the relief of having been let so unwittingly off the
hook by his assumption.

'Well, we'll just have to find ourselves an anonymous
hotel for the time being,' he muttered, as though
thinking aloud.

'We'll *what*?' she demanded in outrage. 'My God,
you didn't actually think I'd be inviting you to stay at
my place if I had one?'

'No, I didn't *actually think*,' he parodied coldly. 'I
was planning on staying there anyway.'

'Tough luck,' she whispered fiercely, suppressing a
violent urge to hit out at him physically. 'I shall be
staying with friends, and——'

'Are you really as stupid as you appear?' he
demanded, genuine puzzlement for an instant warming
the glacial blue of his eyes before being frozen out. 'I
want you where I can keep tabs on you until I've found

my sister. So you can forget about friends, because no one, absolutely no one, is even to know you're back in London. . . Do I make myself clear?'

Penny felt her body go completely limp—a feeling caused no doubt by shock, she informed herself, but one she nevertheless almost welcomed. On and off she had doubted his sanity. . .and now she was convinced beyond all doubt. A man capable of carrying on in the manner he was, and for so trivial a reason, had to be completely out of his head.

'How dare you?' Penny exploded the instant the hotel porter closed the door behind him.

'For God's sake, what are you whinging about now?' demanded Dominic irritably.

'Mr and Mrs John smith!' gibbered Penny. 'I don't think I've ever been so humiliated in my entire life!'

And it hadn't been so much the off-hand insousciance with which he had plucked such blatantly false names from the air when they had registered, as the way his eyes had lingered in appreciative invitation on the extremely attractive receptionist who had appeared unable to take her own openly appreciative eyes off him.

'Just stick around and you will be,' he drawled, picking up the telephone. 'But right now you can make yourself scarce—I have some calls to make.'

'And how, precisely, am I supposed to do that?' she rounded on him, her eyes pointedly flickering round the large double room while studiously avoiding the twin beds dominating it.

'Have a bath, wash your hair. Do what the hell you like, but don't hang around in here!'

Shaking from head to foot with rage, and discovering for the first time in her life what it was to contemplate murder as an attractive option, Penny stormed into the bathroom. When, seconds later, she stormed back out again, he immediately cut off the call he was in the process of making.

'What the hell do you think you're doing?' he demanded, scowling across at her as she dragged a case on to one of the beds and made to open it.

'I need my things——' Her words were cut off as he leapt to his feet, lifted the case and hurled it into the bathroom.

'Right—you've got them,' he snarled, returning once more to the telephone.

Penny slammed, then locked, the bathroom door behind her, hot tears of rage burning down her cheeks as she leaned heavily against it.

She had never in her entire life been treated like this, she raged helplessly. And there was no way she intended staying here with an out and out madman. . .his moods swung with such unpredictable violence that she could well be in physical danger. Not to mention the physical danger *he* could be in, she told herself, scrubbing angrily at her wet cheeks as she turned on the bath taps—his violence was proving alarmingly infectious, judging by what she was beginning to feel sorely tempted to inflict on him!

The choked sob escaping her turned to a groan of pure frustration. Why on earth should she be crying? She hadn't cried over losing her job, nor her home, nor even Rupert, for heaven's sake! Not that Rupert was worth shedding a single tear over, she reminded herself as she sank down on to the softness of the bath mat, her tears unabated. So why these waterworks over a sadistic madman whom she loathed?

It was the sudden and heavy pounding on the door that brought an abrupt end to the increased flood which that last thought had produced.

'What?' she shrieked hysterically. 'I'm in the bath!'

She didn't care if the whole hotel—the whole of London, for that matter—heard her.

'I'm just going down to the foyer,' Dominic called. 'I doubt if I'll be long.'

Of course he wouldn't, she told herself savagely, reaching over and turning off the taps. It shouldn't take him more than a few seconds to finish off what he had started with the simpering receptionist!

Completely panicked by the unavoidable conclusion that her spontaneous reaction had been one of almost violent jealousy, she clamped her hands to her head as though offering her mind physical aid in restoring itself to sanity.

Sarah! She leapt to her feet and raced to the bedroom, almost tearing open her second case. Sarah and her husband Jake had recently moved to a new house in Surrey. Finding her address book, she sat down on one of the beds and searched through it, an almost animal squeal of terror starting in her throat as she heard the firm tread of footsteps in the corridor outside. Holding her breath and poised to flee back to the bathroom, she waited, the breath squeezing out of her in a stifled groan as the footsteps strode on.

With trembling fingers, she dialled Sarah's number.

'Please, Sarah. . .please be there,' she chanted, her vocal cords momentarily freezing with shock when her plea was finally answered.

'Sarah? Oh, Sarah, it's Penny!'

'Penny, you'll have to speak up, love, I have builders all over the place knocking down walls and. . . Penny?'

'Sarah, I can't shout,' whispered Penny frantically.

'Hang on, then—I'll see if I can quieten this lot.'

Her eyes glued in terror to the door she felt sure would burst open at any moment, Penny waited for what seemed like an eternity.

'That's better! Now, what can I do for you?' came

Sarah's breezy tones. 'As long as it's not a bed, though,' she laughed. 'Jake and I are already having to camp in the cellar—it's murder here!'

As her friend chortled happily, Penny stifled a groan of despair—a bed had been one of her hopes.

'Penny, are you ringing from Mallorca? Lexy told me——'

'I'm in London. Sarah, do you know where Lexy is?'

'I thought she'd be in Mallorca with you by now,' said Sarah. 'Penny, is something wrong?' she added anxiously.

'Sarah, I haven't the time to explain. . . When did you last see Lexy?'

'I haven't seen her since the last time the three of us got together, but she rang me. . . I think it was the day you were leaving for Mallorca——'

'You've heard nothing since?' demanded Penny, her heart beginning to pound frantically when she realised how loudly she had raised her voice.

'No—Penny, what's going on? I had a call out of the blue from Lexy's brother the other day, also asking——'

'Sarah, I haven't much time to explain,' cut in Penny desperately. 'But I'm with him now, and——'

'With the delectable Libran Dominic?' chuckled Sarah.

'Sarah, he's a raving nutcase,' protested Penny. 'Lexy's become involved with a man he doesn't like——'

'Lexy's got a new man?' exclaimed Sarah. 'Do we know him?'

'His name's Peter Langton, and——'

'*Who*?' bellowed Sarah, so loudly that Penny found herself cupping the receiver to deaden the sound.

'Peter——'

'For God's sake, Penny, I heard you,' protested

Sarah, her voice harsh with shock. 'Doesn't that name mean *anything* to you?'

'No. Lexy simply told me——'

'Lexy *told* you?' shrieked Sarah in disbelief.

'Sarah, for God's sake tell me what's going on!' begged Penny, her scalp suddenly prickling. 'Sarah?'

'Sorry, love, I was just thinking,' muttered Sarah, her voice a shaky croak. 'It's just come to me why Lexy chose to give you that bastard's name. . . You were abroad when Erica died.'

Penny gave a small start, half convinced that she had misheard. 'Yes, my mother was ill——'

'Lexy and I had had so much of it all by the time you got back that we couldn't bring ourselves to tell you the whole story. . .there just didn't seem any point burdening you with it, too.'

'Sarah. . .burdening me with what?' asked Penny, scarcely able to produce the words, so parched had her mouth become.

'We actually got to know the name of the bastard who'd started Erica off on drugs. The police knew his name and were pretty damned sure what his game was; but the trouble is there's a world of difference between knowing and producing proof—which the police just couldn't come up with.'

Penny brought her second hand up to support the first in which the receiver was shaking uncontrollably.

'Peter Langton,' she croaked, an irrational part of her praying that Sarah would laugh and tell her to stop being so silly.

'Yes. . .and all I can think is that that crazy idiot Lexy thinks she can somehow come up with the evidence the police couldn't! Penny, doesn't she realise she could be risking her life, tangling with that sort of person?' choked Sarah.

'Lexy was always the brightest of the four of us—

remember?' whispered Penny, desperately trying to offer comfort where there seemed none. 'Oh, Sarah, I was so completely wrong about Dominic. . .but he knows who she's involved with and, believe me, he'll find her—even if he has to tear London apart with his bare hands,' she choked, her trembling knees beginning to buckle beneath her. 'Sarah, I know how frantic you must be feeling, and I hate leaving you in the air like this, but it might be some time before I can contact you again.'

'Penny, you're obviously as much in shock as I am,' stated Sarah, her voice dazed. 'I can't understand why Lexy's brother hasn't already explained all this to you——'

'It's a long story. . . Sarah, I have to go now,' she cut in hastily, again hearing the approaching tread of feet. 'I'll be in touch the moment I have any news.'

She reached the bathroom, closing the door softly behind her just as the key turned in the outer lock. Then she stripped and climbed into the bath, the violent trembling of her body still sending out small ripples of disturbance long after the surface of the water should have smoothed back to stillness.

She was right, Lexy had always been the brightest of the four of them—now the three of them, she reminded herself, her stomach lurching with a sickening dread. Lexy just wasn't the type to take risks unless she was completely sure of what she was doing. Yet she had taken the precaution of mentioning that unmentionable name to the only friend to whom it would mean nothing, she pointed out to herself, a shudder of dread rippling through to her soul. How soon had Lexy expected Dominic to get that name out of her once the need had arisen?

Confused and tormented by the idea that it was her own unpredictable reaction to Dominic that had somehow resulted in her letting her friend down, she bathed and dried herself. Once dressed, she went to the door, only to find herself stalling against opening it.

How could he possibly have thought she would have kept silent even for one instant had she known the true significance of that name?

She took the handle in her hand, again drawing back. Even now she couldn't tell him the truth, she realised with hopelessness and frustration. . .he had expressly forbidden her to let anyone know she was back in London, and the moment his back was turned she had done precisely that.

She wrenched open the door, wondering as she did so just how many more lies she was going to have to tell this man.

He was sitting slumped in a chair, his eyes closed and the starkness of a terrible inner despair etched deeply into his features.

Penny hesitated, her arms folding protectively across her chest in an unconscious warding off of the barrage of emotions slamming into her.

This was no longer the madman of her waking nightmare, but a man racked and tormented by unspeakable fears. And the need in her to comfort him, the urge to take his burden from him and restore him to peace, was a force that stripped from her all considerations of self.

His eyes opened, rising to rest on her with a blood-chilling blankness.

'Did you. . .is there any news?' she stammered, her mind thrown into confusion by the intensity of such alien emotions.

'About Lexy?' he demanded with a bitter travesty of a laugh. 'Why the sudden interest, Penny?'

'Dominic. . .she's like a sister to me,' she pleaded huskily.

'Do I detect a sudden change in your attitude?' he sneered.

'Yes, I——' She broke off as she accepted the utter impossibility of hiding what she now knew from him.

'You what, Penny?' he asked with steely softness.

He didn't even know Sarah, she reasoned frantically, and would no more trust her than he did herself. And she might as well accept the fact that mentioning she had spoken to Sarah was quite likely to make him snap completely.

'Dominic, I. . . I've been thinking,' she blurted out, her voice shaking—as was the rest of her. 'And it suddenly came to me who Peter Langton is.'

'Well, I never,' he drawled, a terrible brightness creeping into the dark depths of his eyes. 'The name just happened to slip your mind—is that it? And now it's come back to you?'

'I know how terrible that must sound, but——'

'God Almighty, what sort of creature are you?' he snarled, leaping to his feet. 'I suppose you'll claim that Erica was also like a sister to you! Yet the name of the man who was the indirect cause of her death just happens to slip your memory now and then. In fact so far into your memory that you could even hear it and accept it as merely that of someone special to Lexy, is that it?' he raged, lunging drunkenly towards her as he caught her by the shoulders and began shaking her furiously. 'You're damned right it's a name that's special to her! One she'll not forget till her dying day!'

With a sudden groan he hurled her from him and sat down heavily on the edge of the bed nearest to him.

'Dear God, what am I saying?' he moaned, burying his face in his hands.

'Dominic, it's going to be all right,' choked Penny,

that alien feeling now overwhelming her as she stumbled to his side and placed her arms around his head, hugging it protectively to her. 'Lexy knows what she's doing,' she whispered huskily, silently praying with all her might that she was right.

For an instant he was still, then his head butted angrily against her, a relentless stream of oaths pouring from him as he freed himself.

'Perhaps I could have comforted myself with that—had I not met you,' he stated with hoarse venom. 'But now all I can think is that if she's stupid enough to have a bloody moron like you as a friend she's stupid enough to do anything.'

Cut to the quick, yet forcing herself not to react, Penny took a deep breath. 'Dominic, I know how worried you——'

'For God's sake stop being so bloody conciliatory!' he bellowed. 'It's more than I can stomach!'

Penny froze; then every shred of control in her snapped.

'That's it!' she shrieked, all hint of compassion deserting her. 'I've had you up to here!' As she spoke she drew a forefinger across her throat, her eyes blazing.

'Fine,' he muttered, rising. 'Just spare me the complication of your offering me sympathy. . . That I can't handle.' As though in a complete daze, he glanced around the room, an expression of distaste creeping over his face. 'God, but this place is depressing!'

'You chose it,' she retorted mechanically, thrown by the sudden switch in him.

'Yes, I did, didn't I?' he muttered, gazing around him and giving a half-shrug that was almost embarrassed. 'But at least I'm not likely to run into anyone I know here.'

He reached out and picked up the telephone as it

rang. 'Monique!' he exclaimed, and proceeded to hold a conversation in rapid-fire French.

Probably to make sure she understood nothing of what was being said, thought Penny irritably; he really was overdoing this cloak-and-dagger routine. Even before she had finished thinking that thought, something in her had begun to freeze. His almost embarrassed shrug when she had mentioned his choosing this place was probably a good indication of his feelings about the exaggerated precautions he was taking. . .yet he was prepared to go to any extreme, however ridiculous it might seem, rather than take any conceivable risk where his sister was concerned. That a man of his intelligence, not to mention fundamental arrogance, was prepared to go to such lengths chilled her to the marrow with its implications of how he must be suffering, yet deep down within her was an inexplicable, almost unassailable conviction that he was wrong. . .that Lexy was in no danger.

'Come on, let's see what sort of food they serve in this dump,' Dominic suggested as he replaced the receiver.

Penny followed him from the room in silence, the peace afforded her by the strength of that inexplicable feeling eroded by the memory of the lies she had told in the rashness of innocence—a memory now suddenly leaping into her mind to haunt her.

It was his disparaging remarks about the place that had triggered off this discomfiting train of thought, she told herself irritably as she looked around her. By her standards this hotel was neat and comfortable and clean, and never, by any stretch of the imagination, a dump. But then, her standards weren't based on the familiarity with five-star establishments his were, she reminded herself edgily—and as she had once led him to believe hers would also be.

The dining-room was small, yet cosy and pleasant, and the food surprisingly good—not that Penny dared comment on it as such; doubtless it would fall far short of the hypercritical standards of a jet-setting Libran, she informed herself sourly.

'This is actually pretty good,' he remarked, glancing up from his plate to break the silence that had hung between them virtually since they had left the room.

Patronising devil, thought Penny, disconcerted to find her disparaging conclusions so promptly overturned.

'Don't tell me this enforced slumming's getting to you already,' he drawled, glowering across the table at her. 'Perhaps it will help you grow up a bit, seeing how the other half lives for a change—though I doubt it.'

Penny slammed down her knife and fork, her face pale with anger.

'Frankly, I'm surprised someone like you is even aware another half exists! *You're* the one strutting around as though there's a bad smell under his nose,' she hissed, though her voice had begun rising ominously. 'And *you're* the one who finds all this so depressingly beneath him. And, if you must know, the only reason I didn't verbally agree with you about how good the food is——'

'Would you mind lowering your voice?' he demanded icily.

'Was because I was momentarily stunned by hearing you actually coming up with words of praise for a change!' she continued relentlessly.

'You misjudge me,' he informed her, his words positively dripping ice. 'It's not so much the setting I find so depressing—though I have to admit I've seen better—as the company with whom I'm obliged to share it.'

Those crushing words were scarcely out of his mouth

before they were joined by the receptionist who had booked them in earlier.

'I've been looking for you, Mr *Smith*,' she cooed, the conspiratorial emphasis she gave to the false name managing to incense Penny out of all proportion.

'Have you, now?' murmured Dominic, his entire demeanour altering as his amused and knowing eyes met those of the hovering young woman. 'And to what purpose?'

The receptionist's eye's flickered momentarily towards Penny, then dismissively away as she gave a breathless little laugh.

'Your luggage has arrived,' she told him—her words, to Penny's furiously critical ears, sounding positively inviting.

'Fine,' stated Dominic, treating her to a megawatt smile. 'Perhaps you'll be good enough to have it sent to the room,' he added, the smile switching off abruptly as he returned his attention to his food.

'For someone who claims not to want to draw attention to himself, you're not making much of a job of it,' observed Penny frigidly, the girl's parting smug look having done nothing for her already grossly disturbed equilibrium.

'Jealous, darling?' he enquired innocently, raising his wine-glass and regarding her over its rim through mocking eyes.

'Like any normal person, I object to being made to look a fool. As you insisted on registering us here as a couple, the least you can do is not pick up other women right under my nose,' seethed Penny.

'If that's the way you feel about it, perhaps you should trot off after her and suggest pistols at dawn,' he drawled, his eyes narrowing as they examined the wine in the glass before them.

'Dominic, I warn you. . . I'm almost at the end of

my tether,' she said, weariness and desperation vying
in her tone. 'I know you find it just about impossible
to accept, but I'm every bit as worried about Lexy as
you are.' She picked up her own glass and drained it,
her hand shaking. Where was that wonderful feeling of
certainty that Lexy would be all right, now? 'If I lose
my temper—which I'm almost certain to do if you
continue making a public spectacle of me like this—
then I guarantee we'll be the complete centre of
everyone's attention.' She began fiddling agitatedly
with her glass as she heard her voice threaten to break,
and took a deep breath before continuing. 'I've no idea
what measures you're taking to find Lexy. . .but all I
want to do is help. Please, Dominic. . . I'll do anything——' She broke off, biting fiercely against her
trembling lower lip.

For several seconds he said nothing, his eyes cold
and watchful.

'Why—because you're bored and feel the urge to do
something?' he sneered, his hand snaking out and
trapping hers heavily against the table-top as she made
to leap to her feet. 'Stay put, Penny,' he ordered
sharply. 'OK, I'll tell you what measures I've taken.'
He waited until the angry tension in her had subsided,
then released her hand. 'I've informed the police—not
that they can do anything, but at least they're on the
alert. And before leaving Formentor I contacted an old
friend who's a barrister here, and he's made arrange-
ments with a network of private detectives. . . I've also
been in touch with others whose contacts are with far
less salubrious networks.' He paused, his fingers toying
restlessly with his napkin. 'And now all I can do is
wait.'

Penny glanced at him uncertainly, a thousand questions clamouring in her mind.

'Dominic, why did you pick an out-of-the-way hotel

like this?' she blurted out, selecting one at complete random. 'I know you said you wouldn't be likely to run into anyone you know here, but——'

'But you think it's a touch on the dramatic side,' he finished for her. 'I'm not so much worried about people I know seeing me—there's no reason why I shouldn't be visiting London; it's more a question of how *I'd* handle running into *them*.' He glanced up, his eyes accusing. 'I imagine it must be almost impossible to exchange pleasantries with old acquaintances when you're worried half out of your mind, and its not something I intend finding out. . .though perhaps you wouldn't understand that, would you, Penny?'

When she gave no reply, he glanced down at his watch.

'I think we'd better have coffee brought up to the room; I'm expecting a number of calls,' he stated, rising. 'I can also find out what sort of wardrobe Monique's packed me for this miserable climate.'

'Monique?' puzzled Penny, as she too rose. 'Good heavens, the luggage that's arrived!' she exclaimed. 'You don't honestly mean to tell me you got Monique to pack clothes and have them sent over here to you?'

'You don't expect me to swan around in a climate like this in shorts and a T-shirt, do you?' he demanded, obviously slightly taken aback by her reaction.

Penny's wry eyes took in the immaculately tailored trousers adorning long, athletic legs, the soft cashmere of the jumper he had drawn on over the heavy richness of an unmistakably silk shirt. Shorts and T-shirt, my foot! she thought ironically. Apart from looking the epitome of sartorial elegance, he also looked warm— and the only warm things she had were a sweat-shirt, now desperately in need of laundering, and the jumper she had borrowed from him!

'I suppose we ought to do something about collecting

your clothes tomorrow,' he mentioned as they left the dining-room.

'But we can't!' exclaimed Penny, caught completely off-guard.

She gave a silent groan of frustration as she felt the colour rush to her cheeks under his sudden intrigued scrutiny.

'You're going to have to face up to loverboy sooner or later,' he drawled. 'If it's to be later, I suggest you sneak in and get a few things while he's out.'

Uncertain as to whether it was with herself or with her taunting companion that she felt the more furious, Penny gave an impatient toss of her head.

'Why bother,' she said airily, 'when I feel like a new winter wardrobe anyway?'

CHAPTER SEVEN

SHE had blown just about every penny she possessed, Penny accused herself, half stunned by the disbelief mounting in her as she sat in a taxi on the way back to the hotel, surrounded by a mountain of purchases.

And there was no excuse whatever for it, she remonstrated with herself with growing dejection; she had simply gone way over the top. All right, so she had staggered from the hotel that morning practically comatose with weariness—Dominic having spent the best part of the night either receiving or making telephone calls; and yes, there had lurked in her mind a mental picture of herself decked out to the nines in the sort of clothes she imagined the women with whom he mixed would be. . .one of whom he believed her to be, she reminded herself with a small shiver of apprehension. And yes, she had enjoyed trying on those clothes, the price of which would have normally sent her scurrying in the opposite direction. But what had possessed her actually to buy some of them?

Moments later she was having to admit what a lift it gave to her sorely battered ego as, snuggled in the luxury of her new cashmere coat, she swept past the receptionist without so much as a glance of acknowledgement, her expensively booted tread light and confident as she made her laden way to the lift.

Once in the lift, it was another matter; her spirits plunged virtually to zero as the realisation of her now virtual penury returned once more to haunt her. She was jobless and homeless and had squandered what to her was not just a small fortune, but practically all she possessed—and why? To lend credibility to a silly and totally unnecessary lie?

By the time she gave a fumbling knock on the room door, she had got around to questioning the motives behind her grand entrance of moments before. . .it had been an act of indescribable pettiness, brought about by nothing other than downright jealousy!

Convinced she was undergoing a disastrous personality change over which she had no iota of control, she walked straight past Dominic as he opened the door to her, an expression of grim withdrawal on her face as she dumped her purchases on the nearest bed.

'Had a pleasant morning's distraction, have you?' he enquired, his eyes glinting their condemnation as they swept along the bed.

'Fabulous!' stated Penny, her eyes glittering their own message. 'There's nothing quite like a spot of conspicuous spending to boost flagging spirits.'

Though it had undoubtedly been her own voice she had heard, there was a part of Penny that wanted to turn and check for the presence of another in the room, steadfastly refusing to believe she herself was capable of making such a crass statement.

'No, I'm sure there isn't. . .for you,' observed Dominic, his tone tight with disgust.

'You seem to have no idea how incredibly hypocritical you sound at times,' she retaliated hotly, his words stinging her to defend what she at heart knew to be indefensible. 'Cushioned by the trappings of wealth as you so obviously are, your sanctimonious remarks don't carry much in the way of weight.'

'Give it a rest, will you, Penny?' he muttered with weary disgust, flinging himself down on the bed he hadn't even got around to sleeping in the night before. 'I've sleep to catch up on while I can. . .and no, in case you're interested, we've had no luck so far in locating Lexy—nor Langton, for that matter.'

Tight-lipped and not trusting herself to speak for fear of what might come out, Penny began putting her new possessions away. There weren't that many of them, she thought—doggedly training her mind to concentrate on them and them alone—considering the small fortune they had cost.

When she had finished, she closed the wardrobe and leaned her head against it, all the confusions and feelings of self-disgust she had been battling to keep at bay now running loose in her.

'Dominic, I know how I must have sounded. . .to be honest, it sounded as horrific to me as it must have to you,' she whispered dejectedly. 'Can't you understand that the only reason I keep coming out with fatuous remarks such as that is because I can't get it through to you how desperately worried I am too about Lexy? The last thing we should be doing is fighting; we should be supporting one another.' There was pleading in her eyes as she turned towards where he lay. 'Dominic, I——' She broke off with a soft exclamation of disbelief and frustration. He was fast asleep.

She tiptoed to the bed and stood gazing down at him. Fully-suited and with his shoes still on, he lay sprawled on his back, both arms curved above his head, his face turned towards her and etched with exhaustion even in sleep.

Yet even in exhaustion he was just about the most truly beautiful man she had ever seen, though beautiful in a way that was undeniably and quite aggressively masculine. Her eyes roamed the length of him, from the tousled darkness of his hair to the gleaming leather tips of his sprawled feet, a nameless, mindless yearning churning hotly within her.

This was ridiculous. . .crazy, she informed herself

with dazed dejection; she was infatuated with this wretched man to such a degree that she was unable to think or act coherently!

Penny turned and flung herself disconsolately down on her own bed, a vivid mental picture of Lexy leaping from nowhere into her mind. It was anxiety over Lexy playing these ghastly tricks on her mind, she told herself, desperately willing calm on the terrible confusion of her thoughts. But Lexy would be all right! There was a closeness between herself, Lexy and Sarah that went beyond the bounds of the tangible and which she knew would bring instinctive awareness to the others if one of them was in danger. . .and, from the start, her fears had been cushioned by a knowing that Lexy would be all right.

She closed her eyes, the frantic pounding of her heart easing under the balm of that feeling which had never really wholly deserted her. The string of catastrophes besetting her recently had left her completely disorientated—which was only to be expected, she now realised. And developing this ludicrous infatuation for a man as dangerous as Dominic was certainly catastrophic—but it would die its natural death once Lexy turned up, of that she was absolutely certain.

She turned restlessly and found Lexy's mischievous face smiling down at her.

'It's not funny,' she heard herself protest irritably. 'If this is the sort of thing that's liable to happen to Leos under stress, the least you could have done was warn me.'

'Falling in love with my beautiful brother?' chuckled Lexy. 'There's nothing you could have done about it. . .it's written in the stars.'

'But I'm not in love with him, you idiot—I'm not even sure that I like him! It's simply a question of a most inconvenient infatuation—and it's all your fault!

But I'm only this cross with you because I know you're
all right. . .'

She awoke from that dream-filled sleep to the shrill
ring of the telephone and to the sight of Dominic
heaving his tall frame almost off the foot of the bed in
his rush to answer it. And with waking, too, came the
sluggish uncertainty of how much had been dreaming
and how much reality.

It was mercifully a long conversation, though
Dominic's contributions to it were no more than the
occasional monosyllabic utterance. But it gave her time
to sort out her thoughts and accept the unpalatable fact
that she was undoubtedly the innocent victim of a most
unwelcome dose of infatuation. . .which he would get
wind of over her dead body!

'Any news?' she asked when he replaced the
receiver. Her faith in her instinctive conviction that
Lexy would be all right was now unassailable—her
friends eventual appearance, safe and sound, was
merely a matter of time. And she wanted that time to
be as brief as possible so that her every link with him
could be severed without delay.

'I suppose there is. . .sort of,' he muttered cagily.

Penny sat bolt upright. 'What do you mean, sort of?'
she demanded.

He rose, ramming his hands into his pockets as he
moodily inspected his feet.

'There's a positive lead on Lexy and a man—though
it's not certain that he's Langton. Unfortunately,
they've had to pull back and have a bit of a re-think,
as it seems there are others covering the same ground
as they are.'

'I don't understand,' whispered Penny, almost holding her breath lest the soliditiy of her conviction be
disturbed.

'Neither do they,' mumbled Dominic wearily, seating

himself down on the edge of his bed, his eyes still on his feet. 'When you're probing around what are the fringes of just about the sickest part of what amounts to the underworld, you can't afford to make mistakes. They're fairly sure these other people asking around have Lexy's well-being in mind, but fairly sure isn't enough to take the risk of confronting them.'

'Lexy has no end of friends,' said Penny. 'And I'm sure a number close enough to start worrying over her disappearance and——'

'I contacted just about every friend she has, before leaving Mallorca,' he interrupted quietly.

'How?' exclaimed Penny. 'You probably wouldn't even know half of them!'

'I don't know ninety per cent of them,' he agreed. 'But Lexy left her address book at my place in Paris the last time she was there. As it was only a duplicate there wasn't any need to rush to return it to her, but I took it with me to Mallorca with the intention of doing so there.'

As he spoke, Penny's attention was only partially on his words. . .the greater part of it was centred solely on Sarah. No, she told herself firmly. Sarah simply wouldn't have the first idea how to initiate such a search. And besides, Sarah knew Dominic was doing everything possible.

'Perhaps it's someone not listed in Lexy's address book,' she suggested, confident that whoever it was it certainly wouldn't be Sarah.

He shrugged, saying nothing as his eyes rose to hers, shrewd and piercing.

'Well, it's certainly nothing to do with me!' she exclaimed in defensive response to a ghostly twinge of guilt despite all her certainty.

'I'm not aware of having implied it has,' Dominic murmured, steel in his look. 'Though I wouldn't care to be in your shoes if it had—the last thing we need is a load of redundant cooks spoiling this particular broth.'

'I'd have thought anything was preferable to it being a load of crooks,' she snapped, then instantly clapped her hand over her mouth in horror at such a thought.

'Why the sudden consternation?' he drawled. 'It's only the truth.'

'I *know* it's the truth,' wailed Penny exasperatedly. 'It's just. . . Heavens, I'm beginning to wonder if you're capable of discussing the weather without turning it into something contentious! Why does any conversation we have always end up sounding like all-out warfare?'

He rose, glancing down at his watch.

'For several reasons,' he replied, his tone almost bored.

'Your downright rudeness being the main one,' she retaliated furiously, swinging her legs off the bed and standing up. 'Quite frankly, I'd prefer it if you dispensed with talking to me altogether.'

'Are you absolutely sure of that?' he enquired, walking round to where she stood and cupping her face in his hands before she had the remotest inkling of what he was about to do. 'I think a much better solution would be for the two of us to hit that sack here and now and get on with doing what promises to come delightfully naturally to us.'

'You——' Her words of outrage were cut short as his mouth descended on hers, impatient in its intimate exploration and exuding utter confidence of its welcome.

It was this casual and altogether humiliating assurance he embodied that forced her to clamp her lips in denial of the welcome they threatened to display and that brought her hands clenched and pummelling against his chest.

'Stop being silly and put your arms around me, Penny,' he coaxed lightly.

'I don't want to!'

'Liar,' he taunted, his arms capturing and stilling her.

'Damn you, Dominic—I hate you!'

'But you want me a good deal more than you'll ever hate me,' he chuckled, falling back on to the bed and carrying her with him. 'In fact, I've a feeling the wanting is what constitutes one of our most irksome problems,' he whispered, his words soft and breathy against her ear. 'So why don't we do the sensible thing and solve that problem?'

'I've heard some corny lines in seduction,' she retorted, frantically turning her face from the seductive search of his lips, 'but that one's really in a class of its own. . . Dominic, stop it!'

'Why?' he muttered, his mouth coaxing on hers, his tongue teasing against her lower lip. 'Instead of hurling abuse at me, why don't you just put your arms around me?' he cajoled, laughter in his voice.

Penny clenched her fists, a silent groan of protest winging its way through her as her treacherous arms strained to obey his teasing suggestion. She was lying sprawled half on top of him, a line of fire burning down the length of her body where it made contact with his.

'Come on, Penny,' he teased. 'Put your arms around me. . .you know you want to.'

'No, I——' She bit back her words of denial just in time, suddenly aware that the upper half of his body had begun undulating gently against hers, the material of his clothes grazing against the prominently taut peaks of her breasts in a way she was finding shockingly erotic.

'What were you about to say?' he murmured with feigned innocence.

'You think this is all a huge joke, don't you?' she accused him in strangled tones, hating him for his ability to play games at a time when every shred of her concentration was on trying to keep her increasingly uncooperative body in check. 'Dominic, for heaven's sake, grow up!' she pleaded, the warm masculine scent of him playing havoc with her already intoxicated senses as her face pressed against him.

'I promise you, I'm as grown up as I'm ever likely to be,' he whispered, his body turning and shifting hers till she was on her back.

He gazed down at her, the sultry gleam in his heavy-lidded eyes contrasting disturbingly with the curiously expressionless set of his features. 'And as for my regarding this as a huge joke. . .just how wrong can you get, Penny?'

He lifted her against him, his mouth taking hers in the slow sensuousness of a kiss completely at variance with the urgent arousal of the body against which his impatiently tightening arms now drew her.

'Please, Penny.' It was the choked softness in his plea that lost her the battle, driving her arms up to cling around his neck and causing her lips to part in guileless welcome to the impassioned search of his.

And, once her resistance was gone, her lips remained locked with his even in that brief instant when faint ghosts of alarm sounded in the recesses of her mind, as he impatiently removed first his jacket and then his tie, before drawing her once more into the seductive haven of his embrace.

'You excite me more than any other woman ever has,' his lips whispered against hers as he then proceeded to remove his shirt to the tune of warning bells now tolling a lot more distinctly within her.

Again it was the gentle seduction of his mouth against hers that stilled her alarm, so befuddling her mind with its sweetness that it was only when he drew away from her to enable himself to draw her top over her head that she became aware of his intention to remove it. And even then her arms rose in acquiescence, allowing him to remove the top completely, the only thought in her head being to get this interruption over and done with so that his lips could return to wreak their heady magic on hers.

Then she felt herself torn between growing alarm and the total intoxication of her senses as once more the ardent play of his mouth was momentarily interrupted by his deft removal of her bra.

'You're more beautiful than any man is capable of imagining,' he whispered huskily, his eyes drinking in the golden softness of her beauty before his mouth began touching and tasting at the base of her throat, then moving on in tantalising moistness to the taut excitement of her breasts.

She clasped his head to her, a small cry catching in her throat as his tongue teased against her aching flesh and her body began swaying in a rhythm of invitation over which she had no control and of which she had scant awareness.

'Penny, I want you,' he exclaimed hoarsely. 'A wanting that began almost from the first moment I saw you. . .and I knew it would be like this, almost from that first moment.'

He lifted his head, his eyes holding hers in their impassioned darkness while his hands slid slowly down to the waistband of her skirt.

'Almost from that first moment, I knew I would hold you naked and eager in my arms.' His hands moved purposefully to the fastening on her skirt. 'Just as you knew it too, didn't you, Penny?'

'Yes, I. . . No!' she cried out in confusion, turning her face away from his and dragging her arms from around him to fling them across her eyes.

She pressed her arms against her eyes in an unconscious gesture of protection. It hadn't been the confidence of his actions that had triggered this terrible panic of alarm in her; and the blatant manifestation of arousal in his body had acted only as a potent aphrodisiac on hers. It had been the pleading softness in his words that had stripped her of her defences—but that softness had only been surface-deep, never gentling his features, never once taming the brittle hardness that had gleamed side by side with the heat of passion in his eyes.

'No?' he echoed, a mocking edge banishing all softness from his tone. 'Yet followed so closely on the heels of an altogether uncharacteristically honest "yes".' He laughed harshly, drawing the protection of her arms from her eyes.

'Yes, I want you,' she stated tonelessly. 'Even I'm not stupid enough to try denying that. But no, unlike you I. . . I happen to believe there has to be something more to lovemaking than the mere gratifying of a physical urge.'

'Has there?' he drawled. 'I really wouldn't know.' He rolled from her on to his back and lay gazing up at the ceiling.

'No, you wouldn't, would you?' she exclaimed bitterly, a bitterness she found oddly devoid of any sense of humiliation but, far more oddly, based on an elusive and completely inexplicable sense of disappointment.

'Exactly what criterion do you use in order to help you decide it's OK for you to make love?' he mused aloud.

Penny sat up, hugging her knees against her chest. She said nothing.

'It can't be love,' he continued blandly. 'I mean, it's not as though you're in love with loverboy. . .are you, Penny?' Undeterred by her silence, he carried on. 'Or perhaps you *thought* you loved him and decided to move in with him on that false——'

'Just stop it, will you?' she exploded. 'If you must know I'm just not capable of making love with a man I dislike!'

'If that's the case, you'd better accept that you like me,' Dominic murmured complacently, rolling on to his stomach and gazing up at her. 'Because you're sure as hell capable of making love to me. . .wouldn't you agree?'

Almost beside herself with fury, Penny was about to leap up and storm off into the bathroom—anywhere to be free of him—when, very much in the nick of time, she remembered the humiliating fact of her near-nakedness. She had to make do with giving him a look which should have killed, but which was still no true reflection of the fury boiling within her.

'Perhaps the best thing is to return to where we left off,' he taunted, his eyes cold. 'Or are you determined to kid yourself it was your will-power that brought an end to the proceedings?'

'Would you mind turning your back?' she hissed. 'I'd like to get dressed.'

'Let me help you,' he offered, rising to kneeling position beside her, his smile evilly mocking as he scooped up her bra on the end of one finger and dangled it provocatively in front of her.

She flung herself at him in a fury to retrieve it, realising her error almost in the first instant of moving.

He caught her by both wrists, his laughter mocking softly in her ears as he forced her back down, his hands trapping her arms high above her head as he leaned over her.

'You really have the most delectable body,' he crooned, his smile stopping short of his eyes as he leaned further over her until the darkly matted hairs of his chest brushed against the tips of her breasts. 'And the most delightfully responsive,' he added in mock-surprise as her nipples leapt to erect attention beneath that barely perceptible touch. 'Which is just as well,' he continued softly as he allowed almost the full weight of his unmistakably aroused body be taken by hers. 'You see, you have exactly the same delightful effect on me.'

Then he slowly lowered his head to hers, his lips hovering the barest of fractions from her own.

'What could be more natural than for us to make love?' he whispered, each movement of his lips bringing them into tantalising contact with hers and sending scorching waves of heat burning through her body. 'Oh, Penny, what could be more natural. . .more exciting?' he breathed, releasing her wrists to cup her face in his hands.

And every nerve in her pulsating body was crying out in agreement with those words, sighing in incoherent agreement with them as her arms wound unconsciously around his neck and began urging his head to lower fully to hers.

It was with a small jolt of disbelief that she felt his mouth resist hers. But it was only when the tentative probe of her tongue against his unyielding lips brought his head jerking back to escape her arms that the calculating coldness of what he was up to finally dawned on her.

'You may congratulate me on this, the second manifestation of my remarkable control,' he stated coldly, rising agilely from the bed. 'But don't ever bank on my ability to perform such a feat again.'

He had almost reached the bathroom before Penny

had begun to stir herself from her shock-induced stupor.

'Perhaps you'd care to join me in a cold shower?' he mocked. 'After which I suggest we see about getting something to eat.'

She was aware that she was toying her way through each course, barely taking more than the odd mouthful from each. But it was what was going on inside her head that rendered her lack of appetite completely immaterial.

It was as though her eyes had developed a will of their own, constantly straying towards the man opposite her. But it was the effect on her of what her eyes were seeing that was scaring the wits out of her. The instant her gaze had alighted on the hands now holding a knife and fork her body was racked by the reliving of those same hands in sensuous exploration against it.

She closed her eyes momentarily, trying to block out what was happening to her, then trained them down towards her plate as she forced herself to take another mouthful of food.

But her eyes strayed again, this time to the mouth that had hungered on hers as her own now relived that same hunger.

This was crazy, obsessive. . .obscene, she thought in dazed panic as that hunger slowly spread throughout her.

And the most astounding—and altogether humiliating—thing of all was the total ease and gusto with which he could tackle food while she was in the throes of this complete disintegration!

Desperate to appear every bit as relaxed as he was, she racked her brains for something to say.

'That phone call you had——' She broke off, her cheeks turning scarlet.

'The one just now?' he enquired.

Penny nodded—the one he had marched stark naked from the shower to take.

'I was wondering when you'd get around to asking about that,' he informed her coolly. 'You appear to have an exceptionally low interest threshold.'

She stared at him in blank incomprehension.

'Considering my sister's supposed to be your best friend, I'd have thought you'd be on tenterhooks to hear what was going on. . .not leaving it until you're halfway through your meal before it even occurs to you to ask.'

Oh, God, here we go again, she thought wearily, cramming food into her mouth to obviate the need to reply. Of course she had been interested in any news the call might have brought; it was just that the sight of him stark naked had thrown her completely when she had earlier handed him the phone. Had she ever thought about the subject it would have been males she would have considered the most likely to be dumbstruck by the force of their desires at the sight of a naked female. . .the idea of the reverse happening to her would never have entered her head. Yet that was precisely what had happened to her in that moment she had turned to place the receiver in his dripping hand.

Suddenly aware of his impatiently censorious look, she hastily swallowed the food to which her parched mouth was reacting for all the world as though it were sawdust.

'Well, are you going to tell me or not?' she demanded.

'No—I'm going to ask you a question,' he replied.

'Does the name Winterton—Neil Winterton—mean anything to you?'

She paused for a moment, then shook her head.

'Well, as far as we know, that's the name of the guy she seems to have been with for the past several days.'

'With him?' breathed Penny, her heart leaping. 'Where?'

He shrugged. 'Nowhere that can be pinpointed as yet. But Winterton——'

'Hang on a minute—I've a feeling I *do* know that name,' she exclaimed, frowning as she tried to concentrate.

The next moment her eyes were widening in disbelief, her concentration scattering as Dominic let fly a string of crystal-clear and utterly foul oaths.

'God Almighty, I don't believe this!' he snarled at her. 'First the name Langton just happens to slip your mind, and now——' His words came to an abrupt halt as the napkin Penny hurled at him caught him in the face.

She leapt to her feet and marched from the dining-room. And when she reached the foyer she marched straight on. It was only when she was in the street, with the sting of rain on her burning cheeks and the bite of wind tearing into her lightly clad body, that her steps faltered to a halt. Now what?

One thing was for sure, she promised herself fervently; she wasn't setting foot back there, to be ranted and sworn at as though she were. . .

'Penny, for heaven's sake stopping playing the *prima donna*,' snapped Dominic, grabbing her by the arm and spinning her round to face him.

'Don't you dare touch me!' she yelled, lashing out at his legs with her foot as she tried to twist free. 'You think you can——' She broke off with a choked scream of fear as he caught her other arm and jerked her viciously against him, his face dark with a terrible rage.

'I can honestly say I've never met a more self-centred bitch than you—and believe me, I've met some,' he intoned with a quietness that sent a sharp shiver of fear through her. 'When my sister is found you'll be free to get on your high horse and stay on it forever more, as far as I'm concerned,' he rasped, shaking her with a brutal disregard of his own strength. 'Until then, everything else is secondary, do you understand? Including you and your selfish tantrums! Now, tell me. . .who is Winterton?'

Stunned by the magnitude of his anger, Penny felt her own drain from her.

'His name's not Neil—I think that's what threw me; it's Niall. Lexy was with him at a party a few weeks ago—at least, I think she was with him——'

'Whose party?'

'Dominic, I can't think when you fling questions at me like that. Just give me a moment to think,' she pleaded.

He released her instantly.

'It was John and Susan Bateman's——'

'Their number's in Lexy's book, but I got no reply from it. What does this Winterton do?'

'I'm pretty sure Lexy said he was a doctor. Dominic, are you certain she's with him?' she asked reluctantly. 'It just doesn't make sense. . . She hardly knows the man.'

'She knew him well enough to go to a party with him.'

'I've told you I'm not even certain she was actually with him,' protested Penny, desperately trying to think back. 'I remember her saying something about his being a friend of a friend. . . For all I know they could just have met up at the party.'

He took her arm. 'Come on, we'd best get inside before you freeze. And it might be an idea to pass this information on—at least we'll have the guy's name right, if nothing else.'

As he led her back into the hotel, Penny found herself able to examine his angry accusations, her own anger remaining dormant as she began to understand how her behaviour might appear to him.

Only once before had she had an intuition as strong as this one she had about Lexy; it had been when she was fifteen and her parents had been involved in an air crash. Before she had had definite word of her parents, and despite knowing that several people had lost their lives in the disaster, there had been an unquestioning certainty within her that her parents were all right. It had been a feeling that had no bearing whatever on wishful thinking, and she had been very much aware how worried the school authorities had been in the face of her unnatural calm in the hours before good news had come through. It had been only in Lexy, Erica and Sarah that she had confided her intuitive knowledge, and all three had instantly understood and accepted it.

She glanced up at Dominic's tense and exhausted profile as he held open the door for her, and found herself wishing with all her heart that he could have been one to understand and gain comfort from such an understanding.

'You look cold,' he said, surprising her with the gentleness of his tone. 'I'll have some cognac sent up with the coffee. . . Would you like that?'

She nodded, a shiver unconnected with the cold skimming along the surface of her flesh. 'Yes, I'd like that very much.'

CHAPTER EIGHT

'DOMINIC, there's something I need to tell you. . .well, try to explain, really.'

He had walked ahead of Penny into the room, and now his tall, athletic frame froze to immobility at her words.

'Dear God, what now?' he exclaimed, swinging round to face her, both alarm and suspicion in his eyes.

'It's nothing for you to be alarmed about,' she said, her heart, despite everything, going out to him as the look in his eyes spoke in volumes of the horrors of his inner torment. 'I. . . Dominic, I just wanted to try to explain the reason behind my appearing relatively unconcerned about Lexy; I know that's how I must seem to you.' She cast him a nervous glance, already having serious doubts over attempting to explain what was essentially inexplicable. 'Though you'll probably end up thinking me an even bigger fool than you already do—if that's possible.'

'Why not try me, Penny?' he suggested abruptly, shaking free of his jacket.

'It's just that I have this feeling—except that it's a lot stronger than that,' she began disjointedly. 'Deep down I seem to know that Lexy's all right.' She gave a soft groan of exasperation as a knock on the door interrupted her.

'That should be the coffee,' he muttered. 'Come in!'

Penny watched as the waiter entered and placed a tray on the table, wondering what on earth had possessed her to start all this. His opinion of her was low

124

enough already. . .any minute now he would be convinced she was stark staring mad!

'Come and sit down and have some of this,' he suggested, flinging himself down on one of the chairs next to the table. 'Or would you rather get out of those clothes first? They look a bit damp.'

Penny shook her head, then joined him. She had started, so she might as well get it over and done with.

'Cream?' he asked as he poured the coffee.

She nodded, feeling totally ill-at-ease with his sudden civility; at least with his open hostility she knew exactly where she stood.

'This. . .feeling you have about Lexy,' he said, passing her a cup. 'I take it you're referring to some sort of sixth sense?'

Almost squirming with embarrassment, Penny nodded. 'I'd hate to give the impression I was claiming to be. . .well, fey, or anything,' she muttered uncomfortably. 'I've only ever had a feeling this strong once before. Dominic, I——' She placed her cup on the table, the utter futility of expecting him to understand crowding in on her. 'Look, I'm sorry. This must all sound like complete gibberish to you. . . It was stupid of me to bring it up.'

'Have a drink of this,' he suggested, passing her a cognac. 'Then you can tell me about the other time you had this strange feeling.'

Her eyes flew to his, certain they would encounter mockery, and lowering in nervous confusion when they found none.

She took a sip from the glass, then told him of her earlier experience concerning her parents.

'Lexy and the others understood,' she finished, feeling less and less at ease with every passing second. 'But the school staff certainly didn't; to them I must have appeared almost callously unconcerned, which they put down to shock.' She took another sip of the brandy. 'I really am sorry to have brought this up with you, Dominic,' she apologised in strained, hollow tones.

'Why?'

'Because. . .probably because examining it forces me to face how completely irrational it is putting such faith in what most would regard as wishful thinking.'

'But it didn't turn out to be wishful thinking where your parents were concerned,' he pointed out quietly.

'Yes, but. . .that doesn't really have any bearing on. . .' She bit back the words as pinpricks of doubt began niggling away at her.

She had started all this in the irrational hope that he might derive some comfort from it, and all she had succeeded in doing was undermine her own certainty.

'I think I should get out of these things,' she stated agitatedly, rising. 'You're right—they are a bit damp.'

'Penny, sit down and finish your drinks,' Dominic urged gently. 'And, if it's any consolation, I don't think you're mad.' He paused as she resumed her seat. 'I can't say I've ever experienced that sort of thing, and to be honest I doubt if I'm the type of person who'd allow himself to be swayed by it if I had. But I envy you your conviction. . . God knows how I envy it.' he sighed, lifting his glass and staring moodily down into its contents. 'You see, beneath the casual surface of our relationship there's a bond between Lexy and me that goes beyond our being brother and sister. . . Obviously the circumstances of our childhood brought it about—with each being virtually all the other had for so long.' He gave an almost embarrassed shrug, then took a sip of his drink. 'The only time I've ever known Lexy really freak out completely was when I was involved in a bad skiing accident, and it's only now that I'm beginning to understand exactly how she must have felt.'

Penny reached over and filled both their cups, unable to find any words that might ease the palpable torment within him as she handed him his.

'When I first started getting worried about Lexy—before Langton's name had ever cropped up—I mentioned the drug scene, as well as kidnapping, as an area of concern,' he continued, staring down into his cup. 'I'd hate to have given the impression that I thought Lexy capable of becoming in any way involved with drug-taking——'

'Of course you didn't give that impression!' exclaimed Penny, horrified that he should even feel the need to make such a statement to her. 'And there's no way she could be tricked into it either. Not after what happened to Erica,' she added quietly.

'You feel Erica was tricked into taking drugs?' he asked, his tone non-committal.

'To be honest—no,' she sighed. 'Not that I know enough about the subject even to know if it's possible to trick someone in that way.' She paused, reluctant to put the thoughts she had always kept buried deep within her into words, but feeling almost compelled to do so. 'Dominic, there are some things even friends can't bring themselves to discuss. . .because a peculiar form of loyalty prevents them. I think that deep down Sarah, Lexy and I came to realise that, of the four of us, what happened to Erica could only have happened to her. I'm not even sure I can put it into words.'

Dominic's eyes met hers, almost commanding her to do so.

'There mere fact that Lexy would never so much as mention her background was indication enough that there was something badly wrong, but there was never that terrible vulnerability in her that there was in Erica. From what you've told me it's obvious to me that it was having you as a constant in her life that made all the difference. But until the quartet Erica had had no one. . .she was passed from pillar to post from when she was tiny. . . The older I get the more I can see how incredibly vulnerable she always was.' Penny broke off, searching for words. 'We had lived virtually in one another's pockets at school, yet once we left we often went for months without meeting up. It made no difference to the friendship—just as I'm certain it wouldn't even if we didn't meet up for years at a stretch. But after what happened to Erica we all felt a terrible collective guilt. In retrospect we felt that perhaps she had needed something a lot more substantial than what we had offered—after all, we were her surrogate family; she need more of us than we gave.'

'That's just what Lexy felt,' agreed Dominic. 'She came over to me in Paris after Erica's death and spent night after night pouring out her guilt and anguish over what had happened. I had hoped she'd got it all out of her system then. . . The last thing I envisaged was her doing something hare-brained like this years later.'

'Dominic, we don't actually know she's doing anything hare-brained,' Penny pointed out gently.

'Precisely how would you choose to describe her involvement with Langton?' he asked grimly.

'But it appears she's not even with him,' protested Penny, feeling more and more confused the more she thought about it.

'No, but it's Langton's name that first cropped up and which keeps cropping up. Believe me, he's around all right.' He rubbed his hands wearily across his face. 'It's the waiting, the constant going round in circles that I'm finding almost impossible to take.'

Penny looked at him helplessly; there was nothing even remotely constructive she could think of to say.

'Perhaps if we watched television. . .or something,'

she suggested tentatively, and wished she hadn't—it sounded so pathetically hopeless.

He gave a soft, half-groaned laugh. 'I must say I'm rather tempted by the "or something",' he murmured, rising. 'But I think I'll take a walk. I did say to Rob—the barrister friend—that I might drop round to his place later.' He reached out and gently ruffled her hair. 'Would you mind taking messages if any of the others happen to ring?'

She nodded, a peculiar choking sensation in her throat as she watched him put on his jacket.

'You'd better take a raincoat,' she said, the sensation in her throat distorting her voice. She coughed, conscious of the open amusement in the look he was giving her. 'I mean. . .it's probably still raining.'

'If you say so, Ma,' he chuckled, taking his raincoat from the wardrobe and waving it teasingly at her as he left.

It had been at the precise moment he had reached out and ruffled her hair—a gentle, affectionate and completely unexpected gesture—that a feeling of recognition of something she was unable to define had leapt within her.

She topped up her now luke-warm coffee, frowning as she drank it, and found herself wondering what exactly the difference was between infatuation and love. She immediately felt slightly queasy. He would be so dangerously easy to love, she thought warily—especially as he had been in those past moments of quietness and honesty.

Penny crashed her cup down on to its saucer. Except that the honesty had not been hers, she reminded herself guiltily. Right from the word go she seemed to have been telling him one lie on top of another—the irony being that she was essentially an honest person.

Tonight she should have undone every single one of

those lies she had told him, she accused herself harshly. . .making no allowance whatever for the fact that the idea simply hadn't crossed her mind at the time.

When he returned she would tell him everything, she vowed, no matter what the cost to her pride.

She awoke to a series of muffled sounds, followed by a more distinct thud and then by a very recognisable stream of whispered oaths.

She sat up, groping for the light-switch.

'Really, Dominic, someone should have washed your mouth out with soap when you were a child,' she complained, her expression turning to one of startled disbelief as the soft light filling the room picked him out sprawled across the bedroom floor. 'My God. . .you're drunk!' she croaked in bewildered accusation.

For an instant his prone body seemed to freeze, then he struggled upright, grinning conspiratorially at her as he proceeded to remove first his raincoat and then his jacket.

'Drunk?' he eventually queried benignly, swaying precariously as he removed first one then the other of his shoes. 'What on earth makes you think I'm drunk?' As he spoke he took a step back, while at the same time attempting to remove his tie. An expression of irritation flitted across his features as he suddenly seemed to collapse backwards against the wardrobe.

'What on earth, indeed,' murmured Penny, trying desperately not to laugh. 'Apart from the fact you're having such difficulty remaining upright.'

'Something which, I suppose, has nothing to do with the fact that the floor is littered with your shoes,' he grumbled, with a grin of such lazy affability that any doubts she might have had were erased. 'I could have broken my neck falling over those in the dark.'

'Stop trying to blame me,' she chuckled, fascinated by the sheer unexpectedness of what she was witnessing. 'You're in what is usually described as a state of inebriation and you might as well own up to it.'

'I'll have you know,' he admonished, while having another stab at removing his tie, 'that according to Lexy—and you know what an expert she is—we Librios——'

'Librans, Dominic,' giggled Penny helplessly.

'Well. . .whatever. We held our drink remarkably well—even when we're completely plastered.'

'As you are now,' she choked through her laughter.

'Have it your own way, darling,' he retorted amiably, at last succeeding in removing his tie and adding it to the heap of clothing amassing at his feet.

Penny held her breath, terrified her laughter would distract him as he commenced the monumental task of removing his socks. But as she watched she felt her silent laughter die in the wake of an almost suffocating surge of love.

This was all she needed, she told herself frantically. The man was as drunk as a lord. . .and here she was, all dewy-eyed over him and deciding she loved him.

But the fact that he was drunk was immaterial, her common sense argued with her panic. She knew enough of him to know that this was a state he would rarely get himself into—and, given what he was going through at the moment, it was something for which he could certainly be excused.

And love was a luminous tenderness in her eyes as she watched his laborious attempts to remove his socks—nudging aside her now-faltering attempts to reject it until it finally took its rightful place as part of her very being.

She had seen Rupert drunk—twice, she began remembering. And twice she had been deeply disturbed by his aggressive ill-humour in that state. Whereas Dominic, who could be so disturbingly aggressive when sober, was the complete opposite now.

'Dominic, what on earth are you doing?' she asked, alarm scattering her thoughts as, having succeeded with his socks, he was now fumbling with the buckle of his belt.

'Whatever it is,' he grinned, 'I'm bound to be doing it with considerable difficulty—given the state I'm in.'

Love and laughter bubbling side by side within her, she watched his painstaking attempts to remove his trousers finally meet with success as they slid down his long, strongly muscled brown legs to his ankles. But when he hooked his thumbs in the waistband of his shorts, her eyes closed.

It was the sound of his falling body that brought her eyes wide open again in consternation.

'Dominic?' She flung herself out of bed. 'Dominic!' she shrieked, racing to his side and almost falling herself as she tripped over a shoe. 'What happened?'

'It must be this drunken state I'm in,' he murmured, his eyes refusing to meet hers. 'Perhaps it would be safer if you finished my undressing for me—my trousers seem to have got themselves caught up round my feet.'

For a split second she gazed down at him uncertainly—he hadn't sounded in the least intoxicated. Then his head rose, his eyes meeting hers as he beamed up at her from what she was convinced could only be an alcoholic daze. Briskly she extricated him from his trousers.

'Are you capable of getting yourself into bed while I put away your clothes?' she asked with an exasperated chuckle.

'Of course I am,' he grinned, staying put.

Penny hung up his clothes and put them away, then stood over him, her hands on her hips.

'So,' she giggled, 'you're capable of getting yourself into bed, are you?'

'Yes. . .but I'd rather be here looking at you,' he murmured angelically. 'With that light behind you, you might just as well not be wearing that nightdress.'

Her cheeks suddenly aflame, Penny leapt out of the line of the light.

'Don't worry,' he cajoled, pulling a droll face. 'You're doubtless aware of the havoc alcohol creates with a man's libido. . .as well as affecting his sense of balance. Penny, would you mind awfully giving me a hand up?'

After several attempts at giving him a hand up, all of which almost resulted in her joining him on the floor, she gave up.

'Dominic, you'll just have to get on your hands and knees,' she giggled, 'and haul yourself up the bed.'

With much humming and hawing and seeking her advice, he eventually succeeded—though it was her bed on to which his body finally sprawled.

'Great,' she murmured drily. 'Now see if you can make it to your own bed.'

'Don't be such a sadist,' he protested, burying his face in her pillow. 'Besides, this was the bed I was aiming for,' he announced, raising his head again. 'For a start it's warm. . .and for another thing it's obvious what a state I'm in.'

'I take it that's your idea of a couple of cogent reasons for turfing me out of my warm bed,' she mumbled, giving in to an irresistible temptation to reach out and stroke his hair.

He caught hold of her hand and drew it down to his cheek, holding it firmly in place.

'It wasn't my intention to turf you out of your bed,' he muttered. 'If you'd given me a chance to finish I'd have explained that I'm worried what might happen to me in my present helpless condition. . . Penny, I really think it would be best if you were to get in the bed with me—in case I fall out of it.'

'Oh, I see,' she replied. 'You're frightened of falling out of bed—is that it?'

'Yes.' He even nodded to give more weight to his affirmation. 'And, of course, you'll be completely safe because you know what alcohol——'

'Does to a man's libido,' she finished for him, her words distorted by laughter. 'Yes, you did mention that a few moments ago.'

'And also, we whatsits. . .hell, Penny, what *is* my wretched star sign?'

'Libra.'

'Well, we're the most peaceful of sleepers in the entire zodiac.'

'Dominic, are you sure you're not making all this up as you go along?' she teased, a love so powerful now welling up in her that she felt she would burst from it.

'I'm allowed to do that because Lexy says I'm very typical of my lot—so whatever I say must apply. . . That's logical, isn't it?'

Penny nodded, suddenly terrified he might start thinking seriously about Lexy and get into a drunken agitation. 'Now, would you mind moving over and getting under the covers—there's hardly any room for me.'

'You're coming in?' he exclaimed enthusiastically— every bit as distracted as she had intended him to be.

'If you're prepared to make some room for me— yes.'

He managed to tip most of the covers on to the floor

in his contortions to accommodate her, and almost joined them in his attempts to retrieve them.

'You see,' he murmured with a contented chuckle, as she managed to catch him just in time. 'I told you I'd need you to stop me falling out.'

By the time she had finished arranging herself to his infuriatingly precise instructions—her body curved at just the right angle to his back and her hand cupping his shoulder exactly as he indicated—she was exhausted.

'You forgot to turn out the light,' he informed her, just as she was silently congratulating herself on her achievement.

'Dominic! The switch is only inches from you,' she groaned.

'I know—but you don't want me falling out of the bed, do you?' he asked, in tones of patient forbearance.

Rolling her eyes in disbelief, Penny hauled herself up, reached over him, and switched off the light.

'And I refuse to go through all that performance of making sure I'm positioned to your precise liking again,' she warned him, her heart turning a crazy welter of somersaults as she nestled against him.

She was mad, she informed herself with exceptional calm, given the fact that her heart had now started pounding in direct competition to the activity going on in her stomach. . .completely and utterly mad.

'Penny?'

'Dominic, I refuse to move so much as a millimetre.'

'I don't want you to move; I merely wanted to ask you a question.'

'OK—what is it?'

'If I were to fall in love with you, would you give me my marching orders instantly. . .or would you perhaps dally with me for a while?'

Penny felt herself draw back from him in a purely reflex movement, her stomach lurching sickeningly.

'Oh, well, I suppose that sudden withdrawal's answer enough,' he sighed theatrically. 'Anyway, I just thought I'd ask.'

'Dominic, if you don't shut up and go to sleep I'm moving over to your bed.' Her words, which she had intended as a threat, had come out so filled with indulgence and love that she immediately found herself giving silent thanks that he was in no state to notice.

'OK, OK! But it shouldn't come as any surprise to you to hear I've my fingers firmly crossed against falling in love with you—I'm far too sensitive a creature to be able to handle the sort of brutality you'd hand out to me.'

Though his words were joking, her instant reaction to them was a desire to shake him back into full consciousness and beg him to take them back.

Of course she was out of her mind, she told herself wretchedly. She had asked herself the difference between love and infatuation—and now she knew. For the first time in her twenty-three years she was in love. . .and so completely and irrevocably that it was going to terrify the wits out of her the moment she got around to collecting those wits enough to examine it. This had all the makings of the blackest of black comedies, she thought in desperation—she, with all her recent hang-ups about being frigid, was in bed with a man she physically desired beyond all reason, and for no other reason than to ensure he didn't fall out of the bed! And only someone entirely heartfree could have joked about falling in love as he just had, she thought on relentlessly. He had escaped love up to now, so who was she to hope for anything different? And all those lies!

She sat up, leaning over him and determinedly

shaking his shoulder—drunk or not he had to be told the truth.

'Dominic,' she whispered urgently.

To her complete surprise she felt his body tense in total rejection to her touch.

'I was rather hoping you were asleep,' he stated brusquely, hunching his shoulder away from her hand.

'I—I'm not,' she stammered, his tone distracting her completely from her earlier determination.

'Well, I think it's about time I took myself off to my own bed,' he announced, heaving himself upright.

'You're not drunk!' she whispered, aghast, the knowledge that he never had been so certain that she found it almost impossible to believe she could have been so deluded.

'You sound disappointed,' he retorted.

'But why on earth did you pretend you were?' she protested, while a powerful surge of physical awareness leapt with devastating suddenness within her.

'You were the one insisting I was drunk,' he pointed out. 'I told you I'd fallen over your damned shoes when I came in. I must have sent one flying across the room as I fell. . .the one that almost brought me down a second time.'

'The one I nearly fell over, too,' she whispered, bedevilled by guilt, yet racked with longing. 'Dominic, I really am sorry I leapt to the wrong conclusion——'

'It was the alacrity with which you leapt to it I found so galling,' he cut in sharply. 'I was eighteen the one and only time I've ever been drunk.'

'I've said I'm sorry!' Penny exclaimed, her suffocating awareness of his proximity sharpening her tone and goading her to antagonism. 'But you've had the last laugh by tricking me into bed with you. . .so now we're quits!'

'No, we're not,' he retorted accusingly. 'I intended

having the last laugh. I can't say I was thrilled to bits
to be accused of being a drunk, but then I began seeing
the funny side of stringing you along. . .imagining your
reaction when you discovered I was in your bed stone-
cold sober.'

'So what went wrong?' she managed to ask, despite
the problems now manifesting themselves concerning
her breathing.

'Unfortunately I wasn't drunk.'

'Unfortunately?' she squeaked, her lungs dithering
between exhaling and inhaling as she uttered the word,
and ending up attempting both simultaneously.

'You've already admitted to knowing what alcohol
can do to a man's libido. . .and yes, unfortunately,
mine happens to be alcohol-free.'

'It's all my fault,' she protested, the terrible tension
in her causing her voice to rise unnaturally. 'I had no
right to assume you were drunk just because you fell
over my shoes.'

'There's no need to get so upset,' he stated, his voice
sounding no more natural than hers. 'You can hardly
be held responsible for my libido. . .well, not entirely.
Anyway, I'd best be off to my own bed, before it runs
completely amok—my libido, I mean,' he muttered,
scarcely coherently, 'not the bed.' He turned, flinging
aside the bedclothes with such force that they slid to
the floor. 'Sorry,' he mumbled, reaching across her to
retrieve them, an action that sent an instant shiver of
response down the length of her body. 'Penny, I. . .
Oh, hell!' he groaned, the covers forgotten as his arms
slid around her and crushed him to her. 'Penny, this
isn't what I intended—you have to believe me,' he
protested distractedly, his lips a bare fraction from hers
as he drew their bodies down till they lay side by side.

'I believe you,' she whispered, her arms rising to

cling around him while his lips began raining impassioned kisses on her face.

'Have you any idea how much I want you?' he asked, the urgent arousal of his body against hers echoing his whispered words and awakening in her a ravening hunger crying out to be assuaged as he pulled her fiercely against him.

His mouth took hers, invading it with the ardent sweetness of his need, then drawing back to groan out soft incoherent words before returning to continue its hotly demanding search.

Then his hands were dragging impatiently at her nightgown, his lips again tearing reluctantly from her to urge her to release him just long enough for him to remove it. And then she was back in his arms, the sensation of her skin against the taut heat of his filling her with a languorous intoxication that sharpened until her body was straining to his almost as though in anger that the demands clamouring so violently within it were not being fulfilled instantly.

'Don't fight me. . .please,' he whispered huskily, lifting and arching her body against his to bury his face against her breasts, his teeth and tongue sending sharp stabs of excitement darting through her as they teased and tormented against her aching flesh.

'I'm not fighting you,' she groaned, violent shudders racking her.

'You are,' he replied, his breath hot against her flesh. 'You're fighting me with your impatience.'

'How can I not be impatient?' she begged incoherently, dragging his head from her as the marauding of his mouth became a pleasure too exquisite for her to bear. 'How can you not be?' she shivered, and immediately clasped his head to her once more.

'Penny, I've never felt less patient in my life,' Dominic breathed huskily. 'But I've wanted you so badly it feels as though I've been waiting a lifetime for you.'

There was a small spark of sanity—only barely surviving—in her that warned her she was in over her depth and should heed the caution contained in his words. But his hands and mouth had begun wreaking their terrible magic on her body, assaulting her senses with pleasures so acute that they were almost akin to pain, and rendering caution an impossibility. He had the feeling he had been waiting all his life for this moment—her body was telling her unequivocally that she had.

Caution and patience the thoughts furthest from her mind, she slid her body downwards against his, a giddy intoxication of excitement blasting through her as he responded to her action with a shuddered groan.

'I've changed my mind,' he murmured distractedly, his hands capturing hers from around him and guiding them to the waistband of his shorts. 'Be as impatient as you like,' he urged as her shaking hands responded by drawing the shorts down over his hips.

'I think I can manage the rest on my own,' he told her with softly breathless laughter, easing back from her.

It was the teasing complicity in his words that momentarily cleared a space in the passion-clouded confusion of her mind. She was behaving for all the world as though she knew what she was doing, she realised dazedly—like a confident, experienced woman for whom the act of love held few mysteries. For an instant she felt panic, harsh and suffocating.

'Dominic, I. . .' she began, but already he had begun taking her back into his arms and, by the time he had returned her fully to them, her words, and even the panic instigating them, had all but been wiped from her mind by the swift renewal of the demanding hunger within her.

She had denied his whispered plea for patience, and the urgent purposefulness with which his powerful body was now dictating to hers left her in no doubt that his patience was no longer on offer.

But the small glimmer of fear that realisation brought was swiftly smothered by the violence of longing leaping within her in the moment he cried out her name as his body took total possession of hers. She felt the breath trapped within her expel in a sharp cry of ecstasy as her body responded in uninhibited welcome to the thrusting invasion of his, the ache within her transforming to a throbbing crescendo of pleasure that swelled to an explosion of innumerable pleasures, each one more intense than the last.

'Dominic!' His name was torn from her in a reflex sob, his answer falling on ears no longer capable of hearing as his body took on a new rhythm and began inflicting that incredible process on hers yet again.

Soft, incoherent cries began pouring from her as she clung to him, her arms imprisoning his head in their loving vice, her legs restless against the powerfully muscled length of his until they curved around them in the vice-like pattern of her arms, her limbs entwining him in their loving traps in response to her subconscious need to hold him ever hers.

Then he cried out her name, a joyous elation filling her as her body responded yet again to the ever-changing demands of his. And this time she sensed the heightened urgency in the wild rhythm of his loving, and heard his hoarse cries mingle with the disjointed softness of hers as she felt the power of his passion explode within her and possess her completely. It was then that she was conscious of experiencing true oneness, her body sharing and reciprocating each savage

peak of ecstasy bombarding his, each shuddered spasm
of fulfilment, then each softly sighing ripple of wonder-
ment as ecstasy subsided to a spent delight.

For a long while they lay locked in one another's
arms, their laboured breaths gradually subsiding to
something almost approaching normality.

Then Dominic eased the weight of his body from
her, rolling over on to his back and taking her with him
in the circle of his arms.

Cocooned in blissful contentment, she snuggled
against him as his lips began nuzzling against her hair.

'Would you believe me if I admitted to being at a
loss for words?' he asked huskily.

Incapable of speech, Penny nodded.

'Was that a yes?'

She nodded again.

'My, what eloquence,' he murmured with a soft,
throaty chuckle.

'If *you're* at a loss for words how do you imagine *I*
feel?' she protested lazily.

'Are you trying to pick a fight with me?' he teased,
rubbing his chin against her head.

This time she shook her head, the beginnings of a
melancholy sadness beginning to encroach on her
beautiful contentment.

'Perhaps I should be picking a fight with you,
though,' he sighed.

'Don't you dare!' she exclaimed, a sudden desperation in her to suspend time and keep them both in this
wondrous vacuum of fulfilment forever.

She moved against him until her cheek was resting
on his and to where her lips could silence his if the
need arose.

'But I was the first. . .wasn't I, Penny?' he demanded
huskily.

'Yes,' she whispered, the sadness gaining increasing hold on her, forcing her towards the bleak contemplation of reality. 'Dominic. . .there's a lot I have to explain——'

'Oh, no you don't,' he interrupted with a lazy chuckle. 'You can call me all the macho chauvinists you like, but I don't want to hear a string of reasons why. . . Just leave me to bask in the knowledge of having been the first.'

CHAPTER NINE

'WAKE up, sleepy little Leo.'

Penny woke up to the caress of those words in her ears and the sight of their enunciator seated on the edge of the bed. And the delightfully sensuous warmth pervading her left her in no doubt that she had awakened in heaven.

'How is it you can remember my star sign, yet not your own?' she queried with drowsy contentment.

'I'm afraid we'll have to puzzle that one out later,' he replied, his laughter soft and inciting to her receptive senses. 'I told Rob I'd be at his chambers around nine, and I'm already running late.'

She struggled to sit up, disappointment swamping her. 'Dominic, do you really——?' She bit back the rest of her words, caution taking over as the last vestiges of sleep began drifting from her.

'Yes, I do—really,' he chuckled softly. 'But I can't say I want to—go, that is.' He gave a groaned laugh as colour instantly pinkened her cheeks, then took her in his arms in a brief hug. 'I knew it would be wiser to leave you a note and slope off,' he sighed, releasing her and rising. 'I'll be back as soon as I can.'

He picked up his raincoat and strode to the door. 'Shall I have coffee sent up to you?'

Penny gazed at him in silent bemusement, her mind refusing to function.

'Right—I'll do that,' he grinned.

For an instant he seemed to hesitate, then shook his head, opened the door and left.

For several seconds Penny's eyes lingered where he had stood.

'I love you,' she stated with unfaltering clarity. 'I love, I love you, I love you!'

She flopped back against the pillows, dizzy and elated with the sheer joy of loving. For several seconds she lay there, trying to cling on to that wondrous feeling as she struggled to ignore the questions beginning to steal into her mind and their accompanying stirrings of apprehension.

All right, she gave in at last, what would his reaction have been had he heard those reckless declarations of love? It was impossible for two people to have shared the magic they had without there being love, she told herself in an attempt to dispel the gnawing, nagging sensation now taking such firm hold within her.

Yet he had shared that magic with others, she reminded herself with brutal objectivity, a bleak chill now threatening to envelope her. And afterwards, she wondered with sick dread, had it been protestations of love as fervent as her own that had driven him from those others?

She rose and ran a bath, breaking off to drink several cups of the coffee he had had sent up to her before taking it.

She wouldn't have been feeling as sickeningly uncertain as this if it hadn't been for all the lies, she fretted. . . Or would she?

For well over two hours her mind see-sawed back and forth, examining all the minutiae of their relationship, sometimes lifting her with hope, but ultimately reducing her to dark despair.

After a long battle with herself she reached out for the phone and dialled Sarah's number. It was the fact that she had no real news about Lexy that had held her back from making the call for so long. . .but it was her desperate need just to hear the comforting sound of a friend's voice that finally drove her to it.

At first she got no reply, and later, when she eventually got an engaged tone, the need in her to hear Sarah's voice had become so urgent that she found herself trying the number with an almost deranged persistence until she at last got through.

'Sarah!' she choked wildly, relief and the threat of tears distorting her voice.

'Oh, Penny, thank God it's you!' groaned Sarah. 'I've just had Jake on the phone to tell me of the run-in he had with Dominic Raphael at a fellow barrister's chambers.'

As the frantic rush of Sarah's words continued Penny felt her legs begin to give way beneath her. She fell weakly on to one of the chairs beside her.

'It's just that being better placed than most, Jake thought he'd put out a few feelers regarding Lexy. . . Penny, he'd no idea they'd clash with those already being put out by her brother and his friends.'

Penny felt the blood drain from her. It simply hadn't occurred to her that Jake, being a barrister like the friend helping Dominic, might try using similar contacts.

'Penny, it just hadn't crossed my mind that you wouldn't have told Dominic you'd been in touch with me,' Sarah was continuing. 'Jakes says he's never witnessed a man have more difficulty trying to hide his fury than Dominic when the penny finally dropped. I've really landed you well and truly in it, haven't I, love?'

Penny's shoulders sagged. 'It's all my own stupid fault,' she sighed. 'You couldn't possibly have been expected to know. But there's one thing I have to ask you,' she exclaimed, her voice pleading. 'Sarah, do you

by any chance have. . .well, a sort of gut feeling about
all this———?'

'That Lexy will be OK?' cut in Sarah.

'Yes.'

'All I can say is thank God you have it too,' breathed
Sarah, relief flooding her voice. 'You can't imagine the
number of times I've wondered if I'm not simply trying
to kid myself.'

Her spirits lifting, Penny decided to put another
question which was preying on her mind. 'Sarah, has
Lexy ever mentioned a Niall Winterton to you?'

'I was going to ask *you* about him,' sighed Sarah.
'Apparently he fits into all this somehow or other—but
I've no idea who he is. Penny, there are times I promise
myself I'll throttle Lexy once she turns up. . .then I
think of Erica. Oh, Penny, I hope to God this feeling
we have is reliable, because———'

'Hang on a minute, will you, Sarah?' asked Penny,
her blood freezing as she heard a key in the door.
'Look, I'll have to ring off now—I'll be in touch as
soon as I can.'

'To spread more of the word around, no doubt,'
came Dominic's coldly drawling voice from the doorway as she replaced the receiver. 'Who were you
spreading it to this time?'

'Dominic, please. . .you have to let me explain.'

'But that would only spoil things,' he drawled,
slinging his coat on the nearest bed as he strolled
towards where she sat. 'I don't like my women open
books,' he murmured, drawing her to her feet. 'A few
lies between lovers adds a bit of spice to a relationship,
or so I've heard.'

'Dominic, why try to hide your anger behind flipp-
ance?' pleaded Penny, his touch confusing and exciting
her.

'How could there possibly be room for anger in me

when my head's filled solely with images of you?' he demanded huskily, reaching out and opening the buttons of her blouse. 'Wild images of you crying out in passion in my arms.'

He slipped the blouse unhurriedly over her shoulders, then down her unresisting arms and off her, his eyes never once rising to hers.

'Dominic, why won't you look at me?' she whispered, the coldness of fear clashing with the heat of longing already ignited in her.

'But I *am* looking,' he murmured, his eyes locked on her body as he slowly removed her bra.

Penny raised her hands to his face, forcing his gaze to hers.

'Dominic, why are you behaving like this?' she pleaded, the hot glow of desire she encountered in his eyes doing little to dispel the chilled knot of fear within her.

'Because I want you, my delectable Penny,' he replied, shrugging free of his jacket and then removing his tie. 'Wasn't last night proof of how desperately I want you?' he whispered, taking her hands and placing them against his shirt, guiding her fingers to the buttons. 'Don't be shy. . .be as uninhibited as you were last night,' he urged, as her hands remained immobile against him.

He cupped her face in his hands and began kissing her. And it was the gentle seduction of his kisses that stilled the frantic voice of warning crying out within her and goaded her fingers to trembling response.

Yes, there had been anger in him—an anger he had found impossible to mask in those few moments after he had entered the room. But the magic was still there between them, she convinced herself as her body began responding with an increasing lack of inhibition to the impatient ardour of his.

'I can't stop wanting you,' he groaned in hoarse protest, lifting her in his arms and carrying her to the bed.

'Don't ever stop!' she entreated, driven by the rage of love within her that promised to conquer not only her every fear, but also his every doubt.

But later, as she lay spent in his arms, Penny recognised those promises for the delusions they were. Last night there had been a sense of sharing between them. Yet this time, though his body had driven hers beyond endurance, and had time and again answered fully each demand its passionate urgings had awoken in her, that beautiful, innately mental sense of sharing had been absent.

And last night he had cradled her in his arms, once passion was spent, and in their sharing of one another's contentment there had even been laughter.

She sat up, gazing down at the man in whose arms she had found ecstasy, and yet who now lay beside her like a remote stranger.

'Dominic,' she begged, her face tense and pale. 'We have to talk.'

His eyes rose to hers, chilling in their remoteness.

'OK—so what do you want to talk about?' he drawled, each icy word cutting into her with the keen sharpness of a razor.

'Dear God, how could you, Dominic?' she whispered, aghast. 'How could you possibly make love to me as you just have, and then——?'

'Believe me, making love to you is something I find exceptionally easy to do.'

Her mind and body recoiling in horror from those taunting words, Penny leapt from the bed and threw on her dressing-gown.

'You have such a beautiful body,' he murmured. 'It

hardly seems fair for you to cover it from eyes as appreciative as mine.'

Her cheeks scarlet, Penny belted the gown as tightly as she possibly could.

'Dominic, please don't do this,' she pleaded hoarsely. 'I know I was wrong to tell you——'

'To tell me what?' He cut through her pleas with undisguised savagery. 'Which of your lies—and something tells me there are many of them—do you feel it was so wrong to tell me? Is there a *right* lie to tell?'

'No, but——'

'Penny, you may spare yourself the bother of confessing. . . I simply have no wish to hear it.' He rose from the bed and gazed irritably around. 'Where's my robe?'

'Hanging on the door,' replied Penny, the words out before her besieged mind had any chance to react to this latest madness assailing it.

She shook her head in stunned bewilderment as he strolled to the door and donned his robe with leisurely detachment. Then she sank down on to one of the chairs, holding her head in her hands as she felt something begin to give way inside her.

'This is crazy,' she whispered dazedly to herself. 'It's completely crazy.'

'I really can't see what your problem is,' he remarked in eerily hearty tones, walking towards her. 'You should start looking at things as they are and stop complicating them with matters that really have no bearing on anything.'

Penny raised dazed and lifeless eyes to the tall figure towering beside her. It was crazy. . .and it was probably all down to her, she reasoned tortuously. It could be that he hadn't just uttered the load of incomprehensible gibberish that her ears told her he had. . .it was more likely a case of her mind having finally cracked.

'I suppose your lack of experience makes it that much harder for you to realise that what you and I have is just about unique,' he continued in tones of calm reason. 'But, believe it or not, sex can often be very much of a hit-and-miss affair to begin with—whereas you and I have managed to hit the jackpot at first go. . .if you'll forgive the metaphor.'

Penny felt herself tense instinctively for what his gradually harshening tone forewarned was about to be unleashed on her.

'I can't foresee any problems in our making the best of what we have going for us while it still lasts,' he drawled softly. 'Especially now that my vague apprehensions that this time I might fall in love have proved quite groundless. . .not that it was ever really a serious possibility.'

Penny crossed her arms tightly around herself, imprisoning the terrible pain within her lest it escape and betray the even more terrible sickness of humiliation with which she was doing battle.

'In fact, all in the garden is lovely—or perhaps it's rosy, I always muddle that one—as far as our relationship is concerned. Incredible sex, no emotional ties. . . Penny, where are you going?' he demanded as she suddenly leapt up and hurled her way past him.

He caught her as she reached the bathroom door, his eyes glittering with an inner satisfaction as they raked over her tense pallor.

'If you wanted to shower, why not say so?' he murmured. 'We can have one together, and after. . .who knows?'

'Get out of here!' she screamed at him, beating with her fists against his chest. 'You unspeakable lout!'

'What on earth's got into you, Penny?' he taunted, catching her by the shoulders and holding her at arm's length. 'You don't seem at all happy—yet I can't for the life of me think why.'

'You've had your revenge, Dominic,' she told him, her body going limp as she exerted every shred of concentration she possessed on regaining control of herself. 'Your intention was obviously to humiliate me, and you've managed to do so in a way you know no other man possibly could. . .perhaps that made your revenge all the sweeter, who knows?' She stepped back from him as he removed his hands from her shoulders and gave a mocking bow. 'Now, if you don't mind, I'd like to shower—alone. And afterwards I intend packing my things and leaving; I've had all I intend taking of you.'

'Brilliant performance, darling,' he drawled. 'You should try the stage. Have your solitary shower, by all means, but as for the packing and leaving, you can forget it—you're going nowhere until I say so.'

Still clinging on to her self-control with all her might, Penny gazed up at him, her head shaking in disbelief.

'You recommend the stage for me, do you, Dominic?' she asked in tones of quiet disgust. 'Well, I recommend a banana republic for you, with you at it's head—you're a born dictator. Unfortunately for you I've had more than I'm prepared to take of your dictatorial ways; I'm going, and unless you plan to bind and gag me——'

'Binding and gagging you being precisely what I should have done the moment we arrived here,' he informed her icily. 'Tell me, Penny, do you still have that nice cosy feeling my sister will be all right?' he demanded, taking a menacing step towards her as she began backing away from him. 'Because, wonder of wonders, I don't!'

'Dominic, for heaven's sake stop this!' she protested,

as her last step back from this threatening approach brought her jammed up against the bath.

'For heaven's sake, Dominic,' he mimicked silkily. 'Do you honestly think that just because I happen to lust after your body I wouldn't break every bone in it if that's what it took to protect my sister from your yakking tongue?'

'Dominic, for God's sake, why won't you let me explain?' she beseeched, hysteria edging into her voice. 'What justification can you possibly feel there is for behaving like this when you refuse to let me explain?'

He gazed down at her distraught face from eyes narrowed and darkened with fury.

'It's quite simple, really,' he intoned with soft venom. 'I have no way of knowing a lie from the truth with you. But I'll give you a truth, for what it's worth. . . Yes, I would take any revenge I could on you, but there's little sweetness in it for me in trying to take it via lovemaking. . .not when my body craves beyond reason that of a woman my mind can't even begin to understand.'

He turned abruptly and walked to the door, pausing there with his back to her.

'And because of this complete inability of mine to fathom what makes your warped little mind tick, I repeat what I said once before: I'm not letting you out of my sight until Lexy is returned safe and sound, or, if you'd like it plainer, I simply don't trust you.'

'Dominic, you can't. . .you can't possibly think I'd do anything to jeopardise Lexy!' she exclaimed in horror.

He swung round, his gaze coldly implacable.

'Try putting yourself in my place,' he suggested harshly. 'And then see what sort of an answer you come up with.'

She did just that as she showered, a sigh of hopelessness and frustration hissing from her as she arrived at the inevitable answer.

But it was his fault, she protested bitterly to herself as she towelled herself dry; if he would only let her explain he would find a completely different answer!

She buried her face in the towel, a terrible feeling of desolation sweeping through her, bringing with it the agonising thought of how things might have been. With a sharp exclamation of impatience with herself, she straightened and folded the towel. Fantasising over what might have been was a complete waste of time, she informed herself harshly. She couldn't have chosen a worse candidate than Dominic on which to squander her love—even under the most ideal of conditions.

She slipped on her dressing-gown, her face pale and drawn. The damage done was irreparable, and the result was that she loved a man who despised her. . .and who despised himself for the desire that still drove his body to seek hers against his will.

She belted the gown tightly round her, bracing herself before going into the bedroom to face him.

He was lying on one of the beds, engrossed in a newspaper.

'Dominic, it was never my intention to make things more difficult for you than they already are,' she stated as he continued to read without once glancing up. 'I give you my word that I shan't make any attempt to leave until Lexy has shown up.

'You give me your word, do you, Penny?' he asked, from behind the paper. 'And that's supposed to mean something, is it?'

'You can take it to mean whatever you like,' she snapped, horrified to feel the hot sting of tears on her cheeks. 'But you may rest assured that I shan't leave.'

'Oh, I'm resting assured all right,' he mocked, lowering the paper. 'Because I have no intention of letting you out of my sight for as long as it takes. But, once I do, *you* may rest assured that you're then free to leave.' His coldly mocking words were followed by a soft chuckle of disbelief as he tossed the paper aside. 'Tears, Penny? Now that really does surprise me,' he drawled. 'Surely they couldn't have been brought on by the thought of being free to leave me?'

'Wrong again, Dominic,' she retorted with naked loathing, as she gathered up her clothes to take into the bathroom—she had no intention of dressing under the gaze of those cruelly mocking eyes. 'That's exactly what they're brought on by—and they're known as tears of joy!'

'You've heard something,' she accused him over dinner.

There had been two phone calls, and since them there had been an edgy, brittle tension in him so palpable that she almost felt she could reach out and touch it.

'Let's just say I'm *waiting* to hear something,' he muttered, his mind seeming only partially on his words as his eyes scanned the room. 'This place seems extraordinarily festive this evening—I wonder what's going on?'

'So that's how you plan getting your revenge on me, is it?' she demanded bitterly. 'By keeping news about Lexy from me.'

'You'll get whatever news there is when it comes,' he retorted. 'It's just that I'm not one to go in for counting chickens prematurely. . . Where's that music coming from?'

Penny ignored his blatant change of subject, and gazed moodily down into her coffee-cup. He was like a cat on hot bricks, and, no matter what his claim, she was certain he was keeping something from her.

'Dominic——'

'Excuse me a moment, will you?' he muttered, rising and leaving the table.

Anger, frustration and a terrible hopelessness besieging her, Penny picked up her cup and drank from it. She was sick and tired of being treated like a pariah. And she was sick and tired of the fact that half the time she almost felt as though she was one. . .in fact, she was sick and tired full stop!

Returning her cup to its saucer, she gazed impatiently around, wondering what he could be up to, when she spotted him in conversation with the head waiter. It was with an almost fatalistic detachment that she noted the familiar erotic excitement stirring in her at the sight of his tall, athletic form silhouetted in the doorway of the dining-room. Well, at least this would soon all be over, she consoled herself, only to find that far from being consoled by such a thought she was filled by crippling sensations of loss and despair.

She turned her eyes hastily away as he wound his way back.

'There's some sort of blues group playing in the conference-room bar—wherever that is,' he announced.

She said nothing. What was she supposed to do, leap up and down for joy?

'As I'm likely to go clean out of my mind if I have to spend any more time gazing at the four walls of the room, I suggest we go and listen to them for a while.'

'*You* go and listen to them—I'm quite happy with the four walls,' snapped Penny.

'Penny, if you want a scene it's fine by me,' Dominic drawled. 'But *we* are going to do the listening together.'

'Do forgive me,' she seethed at him in mounting

anger and frustration. 'I understood you were making a suggestion, not issuing an order. And now you're telling me you'll throw a trantrum if you don't get your own way—is that it?'

'Right first time,' he retorted, his grasp on her arm iron-like as he reached out and hauled her to her feet.

'Just stop this ridiculous behaviour!' she exclaimed angrily, struggling with no success to free herself as he began virtually marching her from the dining-room. 'Because this time the worm has well and truly turned! I don't care how much of a scene you choose to create—I'm going to my bed!'

They had reached the doorway when her words brought him to an abrupt halt, and Penny was aware of every pair of eyes in the room trained on them as he swung her round to face him.

'OK, darling,' he announced in a conspicuously loud voice. 'If that's what you want, back to bed it is.'

He pulled her against him, grinning with evil enjoyment as he slowly began lowering his head to hers.

'You bastard!' she hissed, almost beside herself with rage and humiliation.

'A quite unfounded slur on my lineage—but you can't say I didn't warn you I was no gentleman,' he murmured sweetly. 'So what's it to be—a scene the management will probably be obliged to step in and censor, or the music?'

It was the undisguised arrogance of his complacency that tempted Penny almost beyond endurance to call his bluff as their eyes locked in silent battle; but it was her increasing certainty that he would derive every bit as much pleasure from the scene he would undoubtedly create as from her capitulation that finally restrained her.

'All right,' she hurled at him through painfully clenching teeth.

'All right what?' he enquired, his eyes mocking and insolent.

'You win. Perhaps you'd like me to prostrate myself at your feet and——'

'That won't be necessary,' he cut her off, placing a heavily warning arm around her as he led her away.

But as she walked by his side into the dimly lit room she felt the melancholy sob of the blues surrounding them waft into her soul and resurrect the ghost of what had once been her pride.

Pride was something she had never considered herself to be overly burdened with, she told herself miserably, and remembered having once said as much to Lexy in connection with one of her astrological pronouncements on the subject.

'With your beautiful, sunny nature, you've never had to give it a thought,' Lexy had laughed. 'Everyone loves you. . . All I'm saying is that when it comes to the crunch no Leo sits back and purrs when his or her pride takes a knock. Never in a million years!'

Well, her pride hadn't just taken a knock, she reminded herself bitterly—it had been bludgeoned almost out of existence! But enough was enough. The sixth sense that had remained dormant in her for years now seemed to be working overtime—and it was telling her that this ghastly, agonisingly bittersweet period in her life was about to come to an end. Nothing could stop her loving him, just as nothing could stop the devastation and desolation that such love would inevitably wreak on her future existence. But she certainly didn't intend going down without evening up the score a fraction. And even if it ultimately destroyed her she would go down with the love gnawing away at her like a destructive disease, as a secret known to her and to her alone.

She turned to him, her smile brittle and bright.

'You know, I'm really rather glad I took you up on your charming suggestion that we come here,' she murmured. 'I love this sort of music; let's dance.'

His palpable double-take brought her an inordinate amount of satisfaction, as did the unmistakable gleam of suspicion in those shrewd blue eyes as he led her to the tiny dance-floor and took her into his arms.

The charge between them was instant and powerfully erotic, and she found it the easiest thing in the world to blot out the shocked protests of her mind and let her body melt against the familiarly exciting strength of his.

'Perhaps it's just as well things turned out as they did in the dining-room,' he muttered hoarsely, his body leaping swiftly to urgent life as she wound her arms invitingly round his neck. 'Penny, what exactly are you up to?'

She gave a breathy chuckle, her body revelling outrageously in its effect on his. 'Facing reality—isn't that what the experts usually advise?'

He drew back slightly from her, his eyes wary. Then the wariness drifted aside to make way for the sultry gleam of desire as he lowered his head and placed his cheek against hers.

'One aspect of reality fast making its way clear to me is that it would have saved us a load of hassle if we'd gone straight to the room,' he whispered huskily. 'God, how I want you!'

'Such impatience,' she murmured, her teasing words a mendacious denial of the rage of impatience rampaging within her.

She gave a soft gasp of protest as his hand caught in her hair, tugging her head back until she was gazing up into his scowling face.

'If I rightly remember I once cautioned you against impatience, but it certainly wasn't patience that won out then,' he accused, his body a scorching heat against hers. 'Or perhaps you don't remember?'

'I remember,' she admitted in a voice that shook, acting the thought furthest from her mind as need became a savage ache within her.

'Perhaps it's time we got out of here,' he suggested hoarsely, his eyes burning down into hers.

She nodded, pride no longer a consideration as her mind closed itself to all but love and the overpowering need in her to be able to give physical expression to that love for just one more time—before fate gave its final twist of the knife in her.

CHAPTER TEN

IT WAS to the shrill ring of the phone and the abrupt separation of her body from the warmth against which it lay that Penny awoke.

For several seconds her mind and body did battle, the latter fighting off the attempts of the former to deprive her of the last comforting vestiges of sleep. Then suddenly she was totally awake, her body struggling upright as her ears strained to interpret the terse, monosyllabic utterances which Dominic was making into the mouthpiece as he paced back and forth, tanned and naked and with the receiver jammed tightly against his ear.

'Yes. . .and you're both all right?' he demanded.

Penny watched, a heavy, suffocating tightness in her chest as she tried to gauge from the marbled immobility of his features what answer he might be receiving.

'Yes. . . I understand, of course I do.'

Unable to contain herself any longer, Penny leapt from the bed, her eyes begging for a hint from his.

'Right,' he was saying as he gave a small shake of his head and impatiently motioned her to wait. 'I'll see you then.'

He replaced the receiver and stood for several seconds gazing down at it blankly.

'Lexy. . .just tell me she's safe,' Penny begged hoarsely, a sick fear in her that he would shake his head and tell her the opposite.

'She's safe. . .thank God,' he muttered, sinking down on to the chair behind him with little sign of being aware of having done so.

'Thank God!' echoed Penny with a heartfelt sigh, no more conscious of her own movements than he had been of his as she stumbled to his side and placed her arms around him, cradling his head to her in a spontaneous gesture of love and shared relief. 'For one terrible moment I thought. . .but it doesn't matter, she's all right,' she stammered brokenly, tears streaming down her face as she felt the sudden jolt of a delayed reaction shudder through him. 'It's all over,' she whispered, her hands offering him the silent comfort of love as they stroked gently against his hair.

For an instant she felt his body tense, then he suddenly broke free from her and was on his feet.

'Yep, it seems you were right all along,' he announced with studied jocularity. 'And now, as you say, it's all over.'

Penny stood as though frozen in that instant before he had leapt free of her, her arms curved outwards before her as though still holding him.

'Anyway, they're just about through with the police and I've arranged to meet them at Lexy's place in half an hour,' he stated briskly, his voice drawing away from her as he moved towards the bathroom. 'Perhaps you could arrange to have some breakfast sent up while I have a shower?' he suggested, closing the bathroom door behind him without waiting for an answer.

Stunned, Penny felt her arms drop heavily to her sides. Yes, it was most certainly all over, she told herself numbly. And it had been her intuitive awareness of the imminence of this end that had instigated the almost demented lack of inhibition in her during those tempestuous hours that had filled their night.

She pressed her hand to her mouth, stifling a sob as her passion-bruised lips throbbed to memory-laden life beneath the unintentional pressure of her fingers. Time and again she had given herself to him in the frenzied ardour of love. . .and now it was all over.

She lifted the receiver and mechanically ordered breakfast while her mind dissected the events of these past moments with a brutal, wounding clarity.

Her response to the long-awaited news had been to hold him and share the joy. . .his had been to cut himself from her entirely. He had wanted to share none of it with her, his baldly uninformative statements and puzzling references to 'they' leaving questions crying out to be answered.

She picked up her dressing-gown and put it on, a spasm of pain mixed with mounting disbelief crossing her face as it occurred to her that no mention had been made of her accompanying him to the reunion about to take place.

It had been Lexy's disappearance that had got her into this ghastly mess in the first place, she reminded herself angrily. And she was damned if she wasn't going to be in at the end of it!

With determination setting her features, she got out her cases and began packing them; whatever happened, she wasn't staying in this place a moment longer than she had to.

The waiter had just arrived with the breakfast tray when Dominic emerged from the bathroom, and it was without a word to him that Penny passed him on her way into it, the clothes she intended wearing draped over her arm.

And they exchanged not a single word when, barely ten minutes later, she re-appeared, showered and dressed.

The fact that Lexy was safe had to be some indication that things were taking an upward turn, she told herself, pouring a coffee and drinking it while Dominic finished packing the bag he had brought with him from

Mallorca and the case Monique had had sent over from France. And very soon now it really would all be over. . .and she would be able to embark on getting some semblance of order restored to her life. As that thought, intended to cheer her, began filling her with an aching dread, Dominic straightened suddenly and glanced down at his watch with a frown.

'I'd better ring for a cab from Reception while I'm settling the bill,' he muttered half to himself.

'I'll see you down in the lobby, then,' she stated calmly, her only feeling towards him one of loathing. 'I'm coming with you. . .unless you'd rather I made my own way there?'

Without so much as an acknowledgement that she had spoken, he strode to the door and opened it.

'Right—I'll see you in the lobby,' he flung at her over his shoulder as he walked out.

In the shroud of silence that had descended on them in the taxi, Penny was not only having difficulty keeping her delicate veneer of calm in place, but also the thoughts slipping into her head were making it almost impossible for her to retain a grasp on reality. And it was the almost surrealistic absurdity that two bodies, not long ago locked as one in the frenzy of a mutual ardour that had driven them throughout the hours of the night, could now be sitting in hostile denial of one another and as far apart as was physically possible within the confines of the taxi that her mind was finding it almost impossible to equate. And time and again, as they sped through the traffic, she found herself wondering if the same torrid memories as her own could ever possibly exist in the mind of the cold, remote stranger seated beside her.

No, she told herself with bitter resignation as the cab drew up to their destination—it was as though he had flicked a switch somewhere within him and eliminated her from existence.

It was Sarah who opened the door to them, flinging herself at Penny in an unusual display of emotion and hugging her tightly as Dominic strode in past them.

'Oh, heck, I think I'm in danger of making the most monumental fool of myself,' confided Sarah, verging on tears.

'Don't you dare,' gulped Penny, returning her hug. 'You'll get me going too. Sarah—is Lexy really OK?'

'Lexy? she's fairly blooming—the cow!' chuckled Sarah tearfully. 'Jake and I were given a rather garbled account of what's happened when we arrived a few moments ago . . . but I've a feeling Lexy's a bag of nerves at the prospect of facing her brother. And Niall Winterton doesn't exactly seem thrilled to bits with her, either,' she sighed. 'So I suppose we'd better go in and give her a bit of moral support.' She turned and started walking towards the living-room, giving Penny no chance to put any of the questions begging to be asked.

Dominic and his sister were wrapped in a bear-hug as they entered, while he, at the same time, was subjecting her to a litany of most unbrotherly abuse.

The expression on Jake Marlow's face was one of twinkling amusement as he waved to Penny in greeting and winked conspiratorially at his wife.

'I'd have taken odds on his wringing her neck when he walked in just now,' chuckled Jake when they joined him.

'And he'd have done it with my blessing,' muttered a jaded voice from behind them.

Penny looked round to find a well-built, tawny-haired man stretched out on the sofa behind them. His eyes were darkly ringed from exhaustion and he had what looked like several days' growth of beard on his chin.

'You're Niall Winterton!' she exclaimed, embarrassed that she had had such difficulty recognising him.

'A mere shadow of the healthy specimen you met a few months ago,' he murmured with amused understanding.

'Penny!' shrieked Lexy, dragging herself from her brother's embrace and flinging herself into that of her friend. 'Oh, Penny, I'm sure you've had to bear most of the brunt of all this—can you ever forgive me?'

'She's a fool if she does,' muttered Niall Winterton, almost at the same time as Dominic roared out his sister's name.

'Oh, God, I knew he'd be angry,' whispered Lexy, 'but I didn't expect——'

'Lexy!' roared Dominic a second time. 'You can dispense with these hysterical reunions until you've explained yourself.'

'And you're all on your own, sweetheart,' Niall Winterton informed her with decided satisfaction from his supine position.

Her expression a mixture of alarm and defiance, Lexy stepped back from Penny, her eyes openly pleading as they sought those of the man on the sofa.

'Niall, don't be so rotten, darling. . .you know you wanted that creep put away every bit as much as I did,' she wheedled.

'You mean the police have Langton?' exclaimed Penny.

Lexy nodded triumphantly. 'And with enough evidence against him to be able to throw away the key, they reckon.'

'And might I remind you that while you've been playing Sherlock Holmes, or whatever the hell it is you've been up to, I've been having the place torn

apart looking for you?' demanded her brother frigidly.
'So, start explaining and I warn you it had better be
good because I've been half out of my mind these past
few days over you and your carryings on!'

'On second thoughts, to hell with moral support,'
whispered Sarah. 'I'm going to put on some coffee—
coming?'

'Chicken,' laughed Jake via the corner of his mouth.
'I intend having a ringside seat here; I'm the one who's
experienced the rough edge of Raphael's tongue,
thanks to that hare-brained sister of his—not that I
hold it against him. But it'll be a pleasure to witness
justice being done.'

'I'll join you,' said Penny, following Sarah from the
room as Dominic's and Lexy's voices began rising
heatedly.

'The thing I'll never understand is why she couldn't
have let Dominic know what was going on!' exclaimed
Penny in bewilderment, as Sarah closed the kitchen
door behind them and shut out the verbal free-for-all
erupting in the background.

'You know as well as I do how devious Lexy can be
once she's set her mind on something,' said Sarah.
'Especially when she knows people will try to dissuade
her from whatever it is she's up to.'

Penny said nothing as a bitter voice within her
reminded her of the destructive effect Lexy's actions
had had and were likely to go on having on her own
life.

'Almost from the day Erica died I think Lexy's
always harboured a secret determination to bring
Langton to book,' sighed Sarah. 'Then she met Niall
Winterton and learned he had a cousin who had had a
close shave with drugs—though mercifully she has
responded well to treatment. I'll give you one guess
who introduced her to the habit.'

Penny gave an involuntary shudder as she filled the kettle. One innocent life destroyed and another jeopardised at the hands of this evil man. . .and how many others?

'Unfortunately, Niall confided in Lexy that he'd been keeping tabs on Langton in the hope of one day nailing him. Lexy being Lexy decided to step in and speed things up by offering herself as bait. . .apparently Langton's most partial to women.'

'But Niall must have been out of his mind even to consider such a thing!' exclaimed Penny, horrified.

'The poor devil had no idea what she was up to until it was too late to stop things,' Sarah told her. 'I don't know the ins and outs of it, but I know he was livid when he discovered the lengths Dominic had been driven to by worry. . . It seems he's had just about every petty criminal in London on his pay-roll in an attempt to get information.'

'I suppose it's no wonder Lexy was so ultra-casual about Niall,' said Penny. 'She was barely admitting to knowing him when I met them together at a party.' She glanced sharply at Sarah, surprised to hear her chuckle.

'I'm not too sure how much that has to do with the fact that our Lexy is head over heels in love with the dashing young doctor,' she murmured. 'And, I suspect, has been since pretty soon after she first clapped eyes on him.'

'And how does he feel?'

'I'd say the feeling was definitely mutual,' replied Sarah, her expression suddenly serious. 'But she's certainly more than met her match in this guy; how things turn out is something I wouldn't care to predict.'

'Why ever not?'

'Well, he as good as admitted he was so furious over the dangerous mess she landed them in over Langton that he was almost tempted to wash his hands of her.

And I believe she lied to him and told him Dominic and her friends thought she was away on holiday somewhere and wouldn't worry about her sudden disappearance. . . Perhaps livid is the wrong word to describe his reaction to learning that—I'd say he was almost disgusted enough actually to wash his hand of her entirely over it.'

'But Langton's behind bars,' Penny pointed out. 'Surely that's all that really matters in the end.'

'Yes,' agreed Sarah, then gave a small sigh. 'But I'm beginning to believe that Jake and I really are the exception that proves the rule about the path of true love never running smoothly. Look at your luck with Rupert. . .and I've a nasty feeling Lexy's in for an even rougher time with Niall.'

'Well, you can discount me, that's for sure,' muttered Penny. 'Because I wasn't in love with Rupert. I——' she broke off and, to her complete horror and surprise, burst into tears.

'Penny. . .oh, hell, me and my big mouth!' groaned Sarah, rushing to her side and putting her arms round her. 'Penny, I didn't mean to dredge up Rupert——'

'This honestly has nothing to do with him,' protested Penny, terrified she was about to go to pieces completely. 'It's probably only delayed reaction to. . .to all this,' she choked, making a monumental effort to pull herself together. 'Sarah, I think the only sensible thing is for me to go.'

'Penny, don't be daft. . .of course you can't just up and go!' exclaimed Sarah, giving her an encouraging pat.

'But can't you see what'll happen?' she sobbed. 'Niall Winterton will probably take one look at me—once this embarrassing fit of the weeps is over—and blame it all on poor Lexy. I'll only end up causing even more trouble than there already is between them if I stay!'

'God, that's tortuous reasoning if ever I heard it,' groaned Sarah. 'Are you really sure, love?'

'Absolutely.'

'Look—I'll go and have a word with Jake——'

'No—I'll be OK, honestly. . .I'll ring you tonight.'

It was almost a fortnight later that she rang Sarah—not that she hadn't started dialling the number umpteen times before, it was just that she had never succeeded in completing it. She had tried ringing Lexy, too—had actually dialled the whole number and let it ring. She had tried on three consecutive days in that first week, and each time it had been Dominic's voice that had answered the phone and each time she had hung up, her heart feeling as though it were breaking into impossibly smaller pieces each time she had done so.

'Oh, Penny, we've been so worried about you!' exclaimed Sarah, the undisguised relief in her voice only exacerbating the guilt that had been festering in Penny during every one of those passing days.

'Sarah, I know. . .and I'm so sorry for having done this to you. But I had to get myself sorted out.'

'It doesn't matter, love,' soothed Sarah. 'As long as you're all right. . .Penny, you *are* OK aren't you?'

'I'm fine, Sarah—honestly I am.'

'But what about a job—somewhere to live?' protested Sarah.

'I have both.' And both only temporarily, she reminded herself indifferrently.

'Great! I was just about to ring Lexy and beg a bed for tonight; how about if I saddle myself on you instead?'

'Sarah, I'm sure you had no intention whatever of coming up to London this evening——'

'Penny, I was—I swear! Jake's in France playing in

a bridge tournament for the weekend, and literally ten minutes after he'd left I had a phone call to say that Peggy, his sister, had just produced our first neice— two weeks early. I intend being at the hospital gates at the crack of dawn tomorrow to view the baby. . . You see, I'll be providing her with a second cousin in about seven months' time.'

'Oh, Sarah! Darling, that's fabulous news!' squeaked Penny, her eyes suddenly brimming with tears.

'So am I to take it you'll offer me a bed?'

'Of course, you idiot! Mind you, this place is minute——'

'Penny, the floor will do—just give me the address and I'll be on my way!'

Her hand, as she replaced the receiver, was shaking badly, she noticed with pangs of alarm. Of course it would be, she remonstrated sharply with herself—she was thrilled to bits with the news. Sarah and Jake had been married for almost a year now, and their eagerness to start a family immediately had begun to take on a shade of desperation with Sarah as time had passed.

But there was an increasingly edgy nervousness growing in her as she quickly tidied up the minute flat. As the days of her self-imposed exile had slowly passed the searing agony within her had gradually begun to recede to a more manageable nagging ache. She had rung Sarah convinced that the time to lick her wounds alone was at last behind her; yet now that she was faced with the prospect of facing a friend as close as Sarah doubts about her readiness were already crowding into her mind.

It was shortly before Sarah arrived that she finally managed to pull herself together. It was Sarah she was seeing, for heaven's sake, she reminded herself exasperatedly; cosy, easy-going Sarah who would never bat so much as an eyelid, no matter how big a fool she might make of herself.

'God—you look awful!' was Sarah's candid greeting, before flinging her arms around her and bursting into tears.

'Sarah. . .please, darling,' choked Penny, guiding her into the small living-room and urging her down on to a chair.

'Sorry, love,' muttered Sarah sheepishly. 'It's just that I've been so worried about you, and I've had Lexy on my back almost night and day over my letting you take off like that the day she arrived back.'

'Oh, Sarah, this is terrible. . . I'm so sorry!' groaned Penny, guilt washing over her in tidal waves as she sat down beside her.

'Actually, there's no need to feel too bad,' said Sarah with a small hiccuping laugh as she scrubbed furiously at her cheeks. 'Having the occasional unexpected weep is the only negative symptom I've had from pregnancy so far.' Her face brightening, she gazed around. 'It's nice and cosy here—how long have you had it?'

'About a couple of weeks,' muttered Penny a trifle self-consciously. 'Actually, I'm only flat-sitting here— someone I used to work with had to go to Edinburgh for a month with her new job.'

'And your new job?'

'I'm temping until I find something suitable.'

'I wouldn't have thought there would be much temping for graphic designers,' murmured Sarah, her warm brown eyes narrowing in shrewd watchfulness.

'There isn't—I'm just doing general office work till I find something,' replied Penny, then swiftly changed the subject. 'I've put on some cauliflower cheese; it should be ready in half an hour. . . Will that be OK?'

'Lovely.'

'Would you like tea or something now?'

Sarah shook her head. 'Poor Penny,' she sighed. 'Fate hasn't exactly been treating you with kid gloves during these past weeks.'

Penny smiled wanly. 'At least things can only get better—and your news is the best I've heard in ages. I bet Jake was thrilled.'

'Over the moon,' chuckled Sarah. 'In fact I had to twist his arm not to cancel this bridge trip. . .he's gone all gooey on me!'

'And so he should,' teased Penny. 'And how's Lexy? I've felt just as bad about not contacting her as I have you. . . Have she and Niall sorted things out?'

'I'm honestly not sure,' sighed Sarah. 'Whenever I hear from her all she does is go on about you. . . And as for that brother of hers!' Sarah rolled her eyes in disbelief while Penny felt every nerve in her body tense almost to snapping point. 'Heavens, I know he was in a state over Lexy that day, but when you took off. . .as Jake said, he carried on like a miser who'd just been robbed of all his worldly possessions!'

Penny gave a bitter laugh. 'He was probably annoyed that I'd taken off before he'd had the chance to tell me exactly what he thought of me—not that he hadn't made that perfectly clear anyway.'

'Oh, heck, this seems a right old hornets' nest!' exclaimed Sarah. 'Lexy really managed to land you well and truly in it one way or another, didn't she?'

Penny gave a half-hearted shrug. 'It's all history now.'

'Like hell it is,' stated Sarah quietly. 'Penny, you Lexy and I have never been ones to pry. . .but how can I not pry now? Penny, in all the years I've know you I've never seen you as desperately unhappy as you are now.'

Penny felt her entire body freeze as her mind desperately tried to find suitably joking words that would allay her friend's anxiety. Yet when she opened her mouth and spoke it was the unadorned truth that came out.

'Oh, my God,' whispered Sarah dazedly, when she had finished. 'Talk about out of the frying-pan into the fire!'

'Supper should be ready now,' announced Penny woodenly.

'I'll help dish it up,' offered Sarah, jumping to her feet and following her out into the kitchen. 'Penny, you do realise, don't you, that you'll have to see Dominic and have all this out with him?'

'No, I don't!' exclaimed Penny, her pent-up bitterness and anger exploding into her words. 'You know his reputation as well as I do—so don't let's kid ourselves I'm any different from all the rest of his women. I happened to be available at a time when he was worried and needed distraction—that's all!'

'Penny, you love him and——'

'I don't love him, I hate him!' she protested wildly. 'How could I possibly feel love for a man who thinks nothing of making love to a woman he regards as the lowest of the low?'

'Penny, of course he doesn't! Oh, hell. . .the last thing I wanted was to upset you like this, but——'

'Sarah, please. . . I just don't want to talk about it,' pleaded Penny, feeling as though the fabric of her entire world was about to collapse around her. 'There just isn't anything more to be said.'

'I'll probably spend the whole day with Peggy,' Sarah told her before leaving the flat the next morning. 'They appear to have pretty flexible visiting hours where she is.'

'Fine—give them both my love, and give me a ring before you leave the hospital——'

'Don't worry about food or anything—we can eat out,' Sarah called to her. 'But I'll give you a ring anyway—I've made a note of the number.'

With Sarah's candid remarks very much in mind, Penny spent the hours of the morning in bathing, washing her hair and generally trying to do something about her admittedly ghastly appearance.

But her heart hadn't been wholly in it—and it showed, she decided defeatedly as a glance in the mirror brought her face to face with her efforts.

She looked like a saucer-eyed waif, she informed herself with a groan of disgust, and she had a load of newspapers she should be going through in search of a job rather than wasting her time like this.

An hour later, having gone through all the papers and found nothing even remotely suitable, she was feeling thoroughly dejected, and the sudden ring on the doorbell brought her leaping to her feet with undisguised relief.

Obviously the visiting hours hadn't been quite as flexible as Sarah had believed, she thought as she went to the door, her face brightening at the prospect of Sarah's cheerful company to relieve her growing depression.

'Sarah, you. . .' Her words petered to a croaked halt, her startled features paling visibly.

'Aren't you going to let me in?' enquired Dominic, taller and more broad-shouldered than she had remembered him as he filled the doorway in which he stood.

It was impossible that so many thoughts and sensations could be crowding their way into her mind as they were in this instant, she thought weakly, as her eyes drank their fill of him. It was as though his words had been tangible objects that had shimmered across her skin; and there was love, too, a violent physical presence within her desperately trying to claw its way free from the confines of her body and wrap itself around his.

'Penny?'

'No! I don't want to see you!' she exclaimed in a rush of panic, throwing her full weight against the door as she attempted to slam it closed.

His reaction was to push back with such force that she almost toppled backwards.

'I told you—I don't want to see you!' she protested wildly as he stepped inside and closed the door behind him.

'But I need to see you.'

'And, of course what *you* want takes precedence over everything!'

'Penny, I owe you an apology and I've come to make it,' he stated quietly.

'You owe me nothing, Dominic,' she said, a sudden terrible lethargy sweeping through her that left her trembling and her legs feeling like jelly.

'I disagree,' he informed her grimly. 'Penny, why in God's name didn't you just explain you'd lied to protect Lexy?' he demanded angrily, dragging his fingers through the dark thickness of his hair in a gesture of pure frustration.

'I tried and you wouldn't let me—remember?' she hurled at him bitterly, then turned and fled to the living-room before her legs carried out their threat to collapse beneath her.

'That was much later,' he accused, striding into the living-room after her, his vibrant presence seeming to shrink the already small room to the size of a cubbyhole. 'You could have tried telling me when we were still in Mallorca!'

'It wasn't simply a matter of having told you one lie,' she muttered defensively, while silently praying he would just disappear and leave her to get on with this unpleasant process of her complete mental disintegration on her own. 'I told you a whole string of them.'

'Oh, for heaven's sake!' he exclaimed in disgust. 'You couldn't possibly have believed I wouldn't understand your reluctance to divulge to a total stranger the fact that you'd just lost your job and your boyfriend in rapid succession!'

'Dominic, there isn't anything I wouldn't be prepared to believe you capable of—nothing!' she informed him with a savage bitterness, then added with a sudden weariness. 'But quite frankly I'm not interested; it doesn't really matter, does it?'

'*What* doesn't really matter?' he parried in his usual infuriating manner as he rammed his hands into his coat-pockets and threw himself down heavily on the armchair behind him.

'All right—you came here to apologise. You've done so and I accept it,' she chanted expressionlessly, terrified by the fact that he showed every sign of staying, and even more terrified by the conflict of love and hate in her which was undermining her ability to think.

'And now I can go—is that it, Penny?' he drawled sarcastically, his long, dark-suited legs stretched out before him as he tilted himself further back in the chair.

Penny closed her eyes for fear of the hunger she felt must blaze in them as they openly devoured every inch of him.

'Yes,' she muttered faintly.

'It's funny,' he mused, 'that the one thing I honestly felt you were lying about turned out to be the truth.'

'Dominic, please——'

'There again, until it actually happens to you it's impossible to imagine just how bad it can really be. It's just as well you didn't tell me that you'd come to the villa with a broken heart. . . I'd never have understood.'

Penny's eyes flew open in startled bewilderment, then she gave a small shrug of resignation.

'Why the shrug, Penny?' he asked.

'Half the conversations we've ever had seem to have been conducted at cross-purposes,' she replied, her mind carrying her back to those days when they had first met. 'At the beginning I was convinced you were slightly mad.'

'And now?'

'Nothing's changed,' she stated abruptly, stamping out the wistfulness that had crept into her previous words. She rose, mentally crossing her fingers in the hope that her legs wouldn't let her down. 'I'm afraid I've quite a few things to do.'

'And I shan't keep you from them,' he stated, rising also, then walking over to her. 'By the way, what are you doing for clothing?' he asked, halting scant inches from her.

Totally unnerved by his sudden closeness, Penny gazed up at him, an edge of desperation in her expression as she frantically willed herself not to react.

'Your clothes—most of them are at Lexy's place,' he expanded, his eyes narrowing slightly.

'Yes. . . I know,' she stammered, deducing that if she took the step back her mind was shrieking out for her to take she would probably fall backwards on to the sofa. 'I've been meaning to get them.'

'Why not come round with me now?' he suggested, his words almost coaxing.

She shook her head, that familiar tone, added to his almost suffocating nearness making lucid thought an impossibility.

'No. . .and I suppose a goodbye kiss, for old times, is a non-starter too,' he stated in that familiar biting drawl.

'You once claimed you believed in ending this sort

of thing cleanly,' she lashed out at him in a sudden, searing rage. 'Fair, I believe, was the actual word you used to describe your methods. But you forgot to mention the touch of sadistic humour with which you garnish your so-called fairness, didn't you, Dominic?'

'You're wrong about the cross-purposes,' he hurled back at her, paling with anger. 'You and I converse in different languages! I might once have joked about being on the receiving end of what you're now dishing out to me. . .' He broke off, visibly striving for control. 'But then I could only judge by my own reactions. . .you see, I've never regarded a woman's declaring a love I couldn't return as a cause for hating her.' He paused again, then threw her completely by reaching out and brushing his fingers gently against her cheek. 'Whereas your reaction is obviously quite the reverse. *Adios*, Penny.'

He had almost reached the door by the time her mind had started to digest the implications of those words, and her tentative interpretation of them left her reeling with anger and disbelief.

'To think I actually gave you the benefit of the doubt when you claimed to have come here to apologise!' she accused harshly. 'But all you wanted was to have the last word, wasn't it, Dominic? And you don't care a jot how low you have to stoop in order to have it, either!'

'That's right—I'm just a regular bastard,' he retorted angrily. 'And, now that we're both agreed, I'll be off—and naturally I shall be kicking aside any unfortunate cat I happen to encounter on my way back to Lexy's place. And on my arrival there I shall no doubt reduce the poor girl to a quivering wreck when I inform her what a load of bull I find her precious astrological predictions!'

'That just shows how little you know—Lexy doesn't make predictions.'

'Oh, no? Well, the drivel I was subjected to about Leos and Librans and love everlasting sounded as near as damn it to predictions to me. And as you're no more likely to fall in love with me than I am with Dracula's grandmother——'

'That's just where you're wrong!' she raged, leaping to her feet as her temper deserted her altogether. 'And as for you and Dracula's grandmother—it sounds like the ideal match to me!'

He was back at her side in a couple of angry strides.

'Have you just said that you love me?' he demanded, his tone implying he considered her guilty of the most heinous crime imaginable.

'I'd have thought you'd be thrilled to hear it,' she retaliated savagely, the rage in her making consideration of what she was saying impossible. 'You've always taken such delight in telling me how stupid I am—and what could be more stupid than falling in love with someone like you?'

'That makes me and loverboy that I know of,' he stated, his words dripping scorn. 'How many others do you imagine yourself to be in love with?'

'I don't *imagine* anything!' she almost shrieked at him. 'And I only thought I was in love with Rupert because I didn't know any better! I. . .' She broke off, the sickening realisation dawning on her of exactly what her ranting words were proclaiming.

'Well,' he said, his expression slightly dazed as he took a step nearer to her. 'If you love me and I love you——'

'You? Love me?' she shrieked, trying to take a step away and almost falling back across the sofa. 'I may be stupid, but I'm not deranged! No man could treat a woman he claims to love the way you treated me!'

He reached out and grasped her by the shoulders,

the expression on his face throwing her with its sudden and inexplicable lack of anger.

'So how is a man supposed to behave when he falls in love for the first time in his life—with a woman so apparently self-centred and shallow that the name of the man responsible for the death of one of her closest friends barely registers with her? With a woman whose reaction to dire crisis appears to be to take off on a shopping-spree? With a woman who blabs crucial information to——?'

'But I'm not like that,' she protested hoarsely, all that was fair in her telling her that this terrible picture his words painted of her was the only one he could possibly have seen during that terrible period.

'Penny, I know you're not,' he declared with a sudden weariness. 'I was just trying to get you to understand what governed my behaviour. . .even though there's no way it could ever be excused.'

'But I do understand,' she insisted weakly, the peculiar constricting sensation in her throat distorting her words. 'And I loathed the person I managed to sound like so much I'd probably have treated her even worse than you did.'

'Penny, I——' Dominic broke off, his hands tightening compulsively. 'Hell, I've made such a mess of everything I hardly dare open my mouth for fear of making things even worse!' he exclaimed exasperatedly, suddenly hugging her fiercely to him. 'Penny, I love you, damn it! I love you so much I've been little more than a zombie these past few weeks!'

'That makes things a lot better as far as I'm concerned,' she croaked breathlessly, convinced she was about to be suffocated by this overwhelming surge of happiness before she was allowed any chance to savour it.

'It makes you feel better to hear I've been reduced

to a zombie?' he demanded huskily, easing his hold to tilt her back in his arms, and looking down at her with an expression that only exacerbated her conviction that she would suffocate from this sudden surfeit of happiness.

'No, I. . . Dominic, my mind's just gone on strike!' she protested disjointedly, the ability to express anything even remotely descriptive of what she was feeling deserting her completely.

'Well, I suggest you start negotiations with your mind right away,' he teased with the tender, smiling softness of the love she held wholly responsible for this disconcerting inability she was experiencing. 'Because this zombie is in dire need of being convinced his love is reciprocated.'

'Of course I love you!' she exclaimed with breathless indignation. 'Oh, Dominic, how could you ever have imagined I didn't love you?'

'Keep talking,' he chuckled softly, toppling back on to the sofa and carrying her with him on to his lap. 'A lot more of the same and I might begin to be convinced—almost.'

But it was the impatient, impassioned search of his lips on hers that made it impossible for her to comply with his request. And it was the equally impassioned response his lips received that seemed to make him forget ever having made the request.

'I thought I was supposed to be convincing you of how much I love you,' she gasped through a delirious haze of joy when they at last were forced to take breath.

'Ah. . .well, yes—I've been thinking about that,' he muttered, catching his breath. 'And as all this has been such a traumatic experience for me it's going to take a lifetime to undo the terrible damage done.'

'A lifetime?' she echoed faintly.

'A lifetime of my loving you and you saving me from zombiedom.'

'Zombiedom?' She wasn't even sure if such a word existed, but she knew she was having considerable difficulty in saying it, because of a peculiar lack of co-operation between her mind and her body affecting her speech.

'Or—to put it another way—the only cure is for you to marry me. Will you, my darling?'

It was at that point both her body and mind seemed to seize up on her completely.

'If you'd like me to get down on one knee, just ask,' he said, his lips teasing against hers as though willing them to reply.

'Dominic, I. . . I knew all this was too good to be true,' Penny cried, the words spilling from her in a mad rush. 'I told you other lies! I'm not rich—I've hardly two pennies to rub together!'

'Practically penniless Penny,' he chuckled. 'I know all about that.'

'How can you? You're just saying it! How would you know I wasn't just marrying you for your money?'

'The first I know because I had my darling sister hurling verbal abuse at me for driving you jobless, homeless and probably penniless on to the streets,' he laughed. 'As for the second, if it takes my money to get you to marry me, I'll transfer all I possess to you the instant we're hitched—OK?'

'How can you say that?' she exclaimed, horrified. 'I'd love you even if you were a million pounds in debt! Even if——' She broke off with an exclamation of indignation as her body began experiencing second-hand the laughter racking his. 'Dominic Raphael, you are the most infuriating man I've ever met,' she informed him primly.

'But the one you'll marry,' he insisted through laughter.

It was the thought of a life without him that silenced her with its vision of an unbearable bleakness.

'Penny?'

'Yes. . . I'll marry you,' she whispered unsteadily.

'You don't sound terribly enthusiastic,' he complained, his expression becoming alarmed as he drew back and gazed down at her suddenly withdrawn face.

'I know,' she choked, still reeling from the effect of that thought. 'I've a terrible feeling. . .that I could wake up and find that this was all a dream.'

He gave a soft laugh of relief as he gathered her to him.

'Perhaps a word with your future sister-in-law will convince you,' he teased. 'And I suppose I'll have to stop referring to them as "horrorscopes"—because the one she's concocted for us appears to indicate a blissfully love-filled life for the pair of us.'

'So you're converted to astrology, are you?' she murmured, contentment nudging aside the bleak shadows.

'Oh, no—I didn't say that,' he protested. 'The fact that I'll go on loving you for the rest of my life merely shows that I'm blessed with enough sense to recognise that the lady who sidled up to me and stole my heart from under my partially unsuspecting nose just happens to be perfect for me.'

'But I'm not perfect——'

'No—you're full of the most infuriating imperfections,' he chuckled softly, 'all of which add up to making you utterly perfect for me.'

As she blissfully savoured those words his lips embarked on a path of exploration that sent ripples of a familiar need shivering through her.

'I suppose we ought to do the decent thing and put

our poor astrologer out of her misery,' he murmured distractedly, his hands straying purposefully.

'The decent thing,' she repeated guiltily, attempting to still his hands before it was too late. 'I'm supposed to be her friend, and I haven't even got around to finding out the whole story of her ordeal! And what about Niall?'

'Far be it for me to spoil her telling you the story of her so-called ordeal, which gets daily more fanciful,' Dominic muttered, his hand determined to escape hers. 'And as for Niall, we've remained in touch since I went back to Paris—he'll end up as our brother-in-law for sure when he relents!'

Penny smiled dreamily, then decided it was about time she made a more positive effort regarding his hands.

'I didn't realise you'd gone back to Paris!' she exclaimed, puzzlement postponing that effort a while longer.

'I've been back a week,' he told her. 'It was your phone call to Sarah that started up a chain reaction, so to speak. She rang Lexy, who promptly rang me in Paris. . . I arrived on her doorstep at one o'clock this morning.'

At those words Penny released his hands and wound her arms tightly round his neck, burying her face against his as a welter of emotions threatened to overwhelm her.

'Mind you, it took a second call from Sarah—this morning—before Lexy would give me this address. Penny?' he exclaimed suddenly. 'Darling. . .you're not crying, are you?'

She shook her head, her arms clinging even tighter.

'I'm sorry. . . I don't seem to know what I'm doing,' she choked. 'All I know is that I love you—I love you so much.'

'Just keep on telling me that,' he whispered huskily, his lips tactfully kissing away her tears. 'Now and for the rest of our lives.'

She loosened her throttling hold on his neck, turning her face until his mouth was covering hers.

'I love you, I love you, I love you,' she vowed passionately. 'That's what I told those four hotel walls the morning after we'd first made love. . . I told them out loud.'

'I had a discreetly telepathic conversation with the hotel lift that morning, if you must know,' he chuckled softly.

'The morning after we first made love?' she asked dazedly.

'That very morning.'

'But later you told me there was no chance of your ever loving me——'

'I had my fingers crossed mentally—as I hope you had all those times you swore you loathed me,' he teased, then his face grew serious. 'I loved you then, my sweet Penny, as I do now and as I always shall—which reminds me,' he added decisively, holding her firmly to him while he heaved them both to their feet. 'I think it's about time we got that call to Lexy behind us. . .and then we can see about making that last outstanding dream of mine come true.'

'You've only one?' she asked, leaning against him for support as joy rushed drunkenly to her head.

'Just the one—now that you've made all the rest come true,' he whispered, entwining her fingers in his, then raising them to his lips. 'And it's to be able to hold you in my arms and make love to you. . .and at the same time to speak words of love to you and hear your words of love to me. . . Then I'll honestly be able to claim I'm a man whose every dream has come true.'

STARGAZING

YOUR STAR SIGN: **LIBRA** (September 24th–October 23rd)

LIBRA is the seventh sign of the Zodiac, ruled by the planet Venus and controlled by the element Air. These make you easy-going, peace-loving and charming and sometimes indecisive. You have a basic urge to find the right equilibrium and harmony with people, especially when there is a threat of an argument—to the point of charming the birds out of the trees!

Socially, Librans make excellent hosts and hostesses—you possess a gentle sense of humour and like having a balanced set of scales in general. At home you are likely to be extravagant since everything must be co-ordinated and in the right place.

Your characteristics in love: Romantic and flirtatious, Librans love the idea of being in love and thus often confuse infatuation with the real emotion. However, you can be very diplomatic and pleasant and your love for the good things in life ensures a harmonious relationship with your partner. The best way to a Libran woman's heart are candle-lit dinners and flowers, but be careful not to overdo it; Librans can often feel claustrophobic in a relationship which is too emotionally or physically demanding. Therefore, you are attracted by those who are soft, kind and tactful.

Star signs which are compatible with you: Gemini, **Leo**, **Sagittarius** and **Aquarius** are the most harmonious, while **Aries**, **Cancer** and **Capricorn** can be rather challenging. Partners born under other signs can be compatible, depending on which planets reside in their Houses of Personality and Romance.

What is your star-career? Naturally conscious of people's needs and weighing up the pros and cons in all matters, Librans are happiest in jobs which require a balanced viewpoint and a give-and-take attitude. It's not surprising that practising social skills and communicating comes easily to you—such as public relations, marriage guidance, counselling, art dealing, law and beauty consultancy.

Your colours and birthstones: Librans, with their dislike of clashing colours, find pale shades most visually pleasing. Your birthstones are lapis lazuli and opal; lapis lazuli was called the heavenly stone by the Ancient Egyptians and this blue and gold stone makes a perfectly balanced stone for the Libran. Opal is the stone for hope and justice: the enemy of greed and corruption. Some believe it can open the 'third eye' and is therefore mainly used by mystics to re-inforce their supernatural powers.

LIBRAN ASTRO-FACTFILE

Day of the week: Friday.
Countries: Canada, Japan, Burma, China, Tibet and Argentina.
Flowers: Pansy, white roses, orchids.
Food: Apples and potatoes; Librans like food that appeals to their taste, sense of colour and presentation. Light dishes like soufflés, meringues, syllabub and whisked sponges are particular favourites, especially as they contain their own element: Air!
Health: Librans must be careful not to let indecision get the better of them—otherwise reaching a decision or a final solution could be a frustrating experience! Balance is the key word for your state of mind and general well-being.

You share your star sign with these famous names:

Julie Andrews   Bruce Springsteen
Catherine Deneuve   Christopher Reeve
Brigitte Bardot   Bob Geldof
Jimmy Carter   Roger Moore
Sigourney Weaver   Charlton Heston

COMING IN SEPTEMBER

The eagerly awaited new novel from this internationally bestselling author.
Lying critically injured in hospital, Liz Danvers implores her estranged
daughter to return home and read her diaries. As Sage reads she learns of
painful secrets in her mothers hidden past, and begins to feel compassion and a
reluctant admiration for this woman who had stood so strongly between
herself and the man she once loved. The diaries held the clues to a number of
emotional puzzles, but the biggest mystery of all was why Liz had chosen to
reveal her most secret life to the one person who had every reason to resent and
despise her.

Available: September 1991. Price £4.99

W**O**RLDWIDE

From: Boots, Martins, John Menzies, W.H. Smith,
Woolworths and other paperback stockists.
Also available from Reader Service, Thornton Road,
Croydon Surrey, CR9 3RU

A special gift for Christmas

Four romantic stories by four of your favourite
authors for you to unwrap and enjoy this
Christmas.

Robyn Donald   STORM OVER PARADISE
Catherine George   BRAZILIAN ENCHANTMENT
Emma Goldrick   SMUGGLER'S LOVE
Penny Jordan   SECOND-BEST HUSBAND

Published on 11th October, 1991   Price: £6.40